Sometimes I look at myself and I could weep; if I was the weeping kind. Which I'm not. Forgotten how. Nearly twenty years in this force and what have I got? Detective Sergeant Rockliffe: baby minder. What did I ever do to deserve it? Baby minder. That's what they call them: Rockliffe's Babies.

Rockliffe's Babies

a novel by Simon Raby

from the BBC TV series created by Richard O'Keeffe
based on scripts by Richard O'Keeffe and
Charles Humphreys

GRAFTON BOOKS

A Division of the Collins Publishing Group

LONDON GLASGOW
TORONTO SYDNEY AUCKLAND

Grafton Books
A Division of the Collins Publishing Group
8 Grafton Street, London W1X 3LA

A Grafton Paperback Original 1986

ISBN 0-586-07299-3

Printed and bound in Great Britain by
Collins, Glasgow

Set in Times

1

I look at them, and sometimes I could weep. Babies. Babes in arms. Innocents abroad. In a world that's a lot bigger and a lot nastier than most of them can even dream of – and I should know because I've been at it long enough; like I know there's no copper yet who can say he's seen it all, me included. So what do they know? Not a lot. Next to nothing, some of them. In terms of how devious, how various, how unexpected and how stomach-turning nasty the criminal mind can really be. Time was when I tried to tell them, prepare them, but not now. Because you can't. You can't ever truly prepare somebody for the first time they see the body of a kid who's been sexually assaulted, or looking down the wrong end of a twelve bore. They just have to learn. On their feet. And if they can't learn or they can't take it – well tough titty, they're no use to me, or CID.

Sometimes I look at myself and I could weep; if I was the weeping kind. Which I'm not. Forgotten how. Nearly twenty years in this Force and where have I got? Detective Sergeant Rockliffe: baby minder. What did I ever bloody do to deserve it? Baby minder. That's what they call them: Rockliffe's Babies. Like I'm a bleeding nursemaid, wiping their arses and their snotty noses, all those bright, over-confident, cheeky, over-educated, pig-ignorant, forward, backward, clumsy, loutish, yuppish, fresh-faced innocents who *someone* reckons might just have it in them to move out of uniform and into CID. And it's my job to look after them; nurse them along; *train* them, help them realize their full potential, as Mister Munro, my boss,

5

says – with a sneer on his face. All in two years, maximum. Some of them make it in one, not many though and you can usually tell early on who they're going to be. The rest – two years; two chances at the Board. And if they screw up the second time that's it; goodbye and back to being Feet. Often as not you can tell who they're going to be as well.

Take this present lot. Adams, he'll make it in one – if he wants to. And he knows it. Divisional Assistant Commissioner by the time he's forty, that's where he's going, with his degree and his nice manners and his smooth hands. Thing about Adams is, CID might be too dirty for him. He might just decide to stick in uniform and go that way. And maybe he'd be right to, at that. Which definitely cannot be said about Steve Hood. The sooner he gets into CID the better, because otherwise that nasty jack-boot streak he's got could land him in a lot of bother. Could land him in bother in CID, come to that, but at least there he'd have an outlet for it.

The birds are alright. Little Karen Walsh is a natural if ever I saw one: she's got nous, she's got bottle, she's got initiative. Bit of a loner, maybe, but there are certain kinds of CID work, like going undercover, where that's an up-front, first priority. Janice Hargreaves is completely the oppo. A good team member, a good all-rounder, a bundle of laughs is our Jan – and, by Christ, we could do with a few more black detectives! If she doesn't make it I'll lie down, roll over and put my paws in the air.

The only two out of this lot I've got real question marks about are Keith Chitty and Paul Georgiou. I don't know what to make of Georgiou. Doesn't seem to put himself about much; likes sitting on his arse more than I'd reckon a detective should. He gets the collars, though; enough, somehow; and he's not stupid, so I don't know . . . Chitty, I have deep reservations about. He's already failed one Board and, quite frankly, I can't see it being much different next time round. I can't even work out what he's doing wanting to be a copper at all. I mean, if you had the choice between chewing a straw and tilling the good earth in deepest Dorset and sweeping the garbage out of London's gutters, what would you do? If I was him I wouldn't be here, doing this, I tell you. On top of which, it's not that he's thick – he just seems like it. The bloody irony is, as a thief-taker he's not bad. But that still doesn't solve the problem of the way he looks or the way he sounds or the way he comes across generally. I've tried to tell him, gently as I know how, ask him – what's he *doing* here? Only now I think about it, I'm not sure I've ever had an answer off him. So maybe he doesn't know himself . . .

So: that just leaves O'Dowd. Gerry O'Dowd! What the hell do you say about him? He's a one-off, and no mistake. O'Dowd! He's the stuff that dreams are made of – mine, anyway, and they're nightmares, mostly. O'Dowd! God Bless O'Dowd, and save me from him! If anyone's going to get into deep water on this squad, and drag the rest in with him, you can bet all you want it'll be Gerry O'Dowd . . .

2

It was O'Dowd who spotted the car and decided it was of interest. There was something about it – too new, too clean, too incongruous somehow here in the Dragon, wasteland of high-rise towers, catwalks, balconies and no-go squares of parched, worn grass where a uniformed copper would only patrol at his peril. It didn't fit. So now they waited while he radioed in the details, feeling tired and frustrated and weary at the end of a fruitless day.

Not far away kids were playing around one of the stair-wells and already they were casting glances at the van that betokened a growing curiosity: it had arrived; it had parked; no one had got out.

'Sit here much longer, they're gonna make us,' Hood warned.

'Sitting duck for snipers,' Chitty agreed, somewhat ambiguously.

Adams, in the driving seat, glanced sharply up to the catwalks and the balconies because after Broadwater Farm that wasn't such a joke; but the only thing that moved was an elderly female resident, heading along her balcony towards a stair-well.

Into his PR O'Dowd suddenly said, 'Yeah? . . . Yeah, great! Goddit . . . No, we'll lift him when he comes out. No assistance required.'

The others glanced at each other as he removed his headphones; it sounded suspiciously like his hunch had been proved right – yet again, bugger him! 'Car's an overdue hiring,' he announced with a smirk, 'and fella's of interest to the drugs squad. So we're to pull him.'

'I don't know how you do it,' Adams said.

'I'm just a natural,' O'Dowd rejoined cheerfully.

'Jammy sod, you mean,' Hood grunted, unable to keep the hint of resentment and jealousy out of his voice.

'So what do we do?' Chitty asked, somewhat anxiously.

'Wait,' O'Dowd said.

Chitty groaned. 'I couldn't half do with a leak.'

'Not in here,' Adams said sharply.

Chitty groaned again. 'Bloomin' heck!'

'Tie a knot in it,' Hood suggested, and grinned at the others.

From the nearest of the pedestrian underpass tunnels which honeycombed the estate two more kids had appeared, one white and one black, both on BMXs. They came wheely-ing out on to the grass, competing to stay on one wheel longer than the other, to hoist their front wheels higher, to turn more sharply; like performing ponies in a circus, Adams thought, watching their expertise with something that bordered almost on to awe. Couldn't be more than ten, either of them, yet already such careless confidence and macho bravura . . .

'Hey, look at those two,' he said.

His timing couldn't have been better. The old lady from the flats above had emerged from her stair-well and was heading for the nearest tunnel. The boys had seen her and, even as Chitty, O'Dowd and Hood turned to look, they were weaving their bikes around her, tighter and tighter, hemming her in. She stopped and shooed at them, waving her arms and handbag as though shooing away a dog but it had no effect. Instead the black boy of the pair planted his bike directly across her path while his white compatriot made a sudden grab for the woman's handbag. For a moment the four young coppers in the van were too astonished to react. Incredulously they watched as a tug-of-war developed between the boy and the old lady over her handbag.

'Seen everything now,' Hood said. 'Broad daylight and all.'

The old lady didn't really stand much chance. In a moment the boy had wrested the bag from her grasp and was tantalizingly holding it just out of her reach. Then he lobbed it to his mate who immediately took off on his bike.

For Chitty, that was it. 'Right,' he said. It galvanized the others into action. Hood threw open the back doors of the van and he and Chitty dived out. Adams rolled back the driver's door and joined them as they raced across the green. O'Dowd, as Communications Officer, stayed put, watching as they plunged down into the tunnel after the black boy on his bike. He looked to the suspect car and offered a silent prayer that nothing developed until the others got back or – even more important – that they hadn't already blown their presence. Movement over at the entrance to the tunnel once more caught his eye. The black boy was cycling back out again, still holding the handbag; but where were Hood, Chitty and Adams? . . .

'Christ, you wouldn't believe it,' O'Dowd said to himself. Where *were* they?! The black boy was cycling right past the van. Somehow or other he must have doubled back without them realizing so now they were going in one direction and he was going in completely the opposite. Another second or two and he would be clear away! Desperately O'Dowd looked for the others, willing them to appear; but they didn't, so it was up to him, one way or the other.

The rules were very clear: *never* in a hostile environment leave the van unattended. O'Dowd broke the rules, and knew that he was doing so. But, as he said later, there didn't seem, at the time, to be all that much choice. He launched himself out of the back doors of the van and took off after the black kid with a yell.

'Hey, you!! No, you don't!!'

As far as the kid on the BMX was concerned, O'Dowd had appeared out of nowhere and it panicked him. He swerved sharply back towards the flats, back towards the stair-well. O'Dowd veered after him, cutting across the corner the boy's turn had made and gaining on him. The boy saw the bulk of building looming in his path and tried to turn again. But this time O'Dowd had anticipated him and had already slanted right. The boy wrenched his wheel back over to the left and for an instant it looked as though he was going to come off the bike, but long hours practising wheelies and seemingly impossible stunts kept him astride it . . . to no avail. Because he had run out of room to manoeuvre. He was cornered in the angle between the stair-well and the wall against which the refuse bins were lined, and he had nowhere left to go.

Trapped and suddenly very frightened he looked back to O'Dowd who, panting, was now slowly, menacingly, closing on him.

'It was a joke, Mister! . . .'

'Shut your face.'

'I done nothing! It was him! . . .'

The boy started to cry and suddenly looked his age. All the bravura had gone out of him and he was just a naughty kid, terrified and self-pitying. O'Dowd could feel himself involuntarily softening. It almost annoyed him, but he couldn't help it. He said, 'Come on, son.' At which the boy just threw the bag down at his feet and O'Dowd bent to pick it up.

As he did so he heard Chitty's shout: 'Gerry! . . .' And there was more than just urgency in it – panic, almost.

O'Dowd looked round. Adams and Hood were with

11

the old lady. Chitty, a little apart, was pointing across the grass to the road, to the suspect car, where a man and a woman were climbing into it: too far away at this distance to make out more than that he was black and she was white. O'Dowd suddenly went hot and felt sick. 'Jesus,' he said, and started running.

The kid on his BMX watched in blurred amazement. The belting he had been expecting was receding away from him as fast as the bloke's legs could run. Now, the kid didn't believe in providence; wouldn't have known what you were talking about if you had mentioned it to him. But he did know a lucky break when he saw one, and this was definitely one ace, lucky break! He didn't wait for the bloke to have second thoughts; he hoisted himself on to his bike and took off for the tunnels like all the hounds of hell were at his heels.

O'Dowd was the last one back to the van and Adams was already gunning the engine as he scrambled into the back, dragging the doors closed behind him. The suspect car had passed, cheekily, right by them and was approaching the main road but the van was pointing in the wrong direction to follow, so Adams slammed it up over the kerb on to the grass, turning it in a bouncing, tilting circle. For a brief moment the bouncing and the tilting seemed natural; but once the van had straightened and they were still bouncing and tilting, and there was a rhythmic thudding coming from their near side, it began to dawn on them that something wasn't right.

Adams stopped the van. Urgently, they spilled back out again. Previously unseen, the word 'Filth' had been aerosol sprayed on the van's side, and both of the near side wheels had been punctured. Helplessly, grimly, they looked around. The suspect car had disappeared. And of the gaggle of kids who had been

12

playing near to the stair-well when they arrived there was now not a sign.

O'Dowd caught most of the flak for that one. He should never have left the van unattended. The result of his having done so: damage to the van's axles caused by riding the kerb and what might have been a good collar lost. All well and good for O'Dowd to plead that he had only done it on impulse; the trouble was, his 'impulses' were becoming somewhat notorious. Which made it all the more imperative that he didn't screw up on the next job!

It was a stake-out of a building society which, going by the pattern previously established, was likely to be the next target of a lone, armed robber who, obligingly, only seemed to operate on Wednesday afternoons. Since his average take was less than three hundred it seemed likely he was just a smack-head doing what was necessary in order to maintain his habit. The most worrying feature about him was his gun: not a shotgun, just a small hand-held; but still no way yet of knowing whether it was real or imitation, or what might happen if he was dangerously unstable and was spooked. DI Flight's instructions, therefore, were very precise. If he showed, no one was to tackle him. Flight himself and Chitty were to leave their observation point, get into the car and, on the man's departure from the building society, get ahead of him. Only then were O'Dowd and Hood to close in from behind.

The observation/command post was an upstairs room above a junk shop, directly opposite the building society. Hood and O'Dowd were on the street below, trying not to look conspicuous as they waited. Fortunately, it was busy enough for them not to stand out, though the thought of shots being fired in a crowded shopping street caused DI Flight's ticker to have mild palpitations.

From his position behind the grimy net curtain at the window he could see Hood and O'Dowd quite clearly. For some reason which escaped him, O'Dowd seemed to be more interested in the junk shop than in the building society.

'Mind's all over the place, that lad,' he observed, almost to himself.

'No, sir,' Chitty responded drily. 'Always on the same place.'

Flight looked at him, not understanding.

'Reckons he's in with a chance with that young lady downstairs,' Chitty explained. 'Reckons she fancies him.'

Flight groaned, and closed his eyes in despair. But then he opened them again fast as Chitty suddenly nudged him.

'What? . . .'

Chitty nodded out to the street. 'Second time he's been past.'

He was indicating an Asian man, in his twenties, carrying a plastic carrier bag and with a scarf obscuring most of his lower face. He fitted their description in all respects but one.

'No combat jacket,' Flight said.

'Perhaps he's lashed out,' Chitty replied.

Flight picked up his PR. 'One-Five or One-Three. Have you clocked him? Paki with the carrier, over?'

It was Hood who responded. 'Victor One-Five here, Victor One-Zero. One-Three's body set's packed up.'

'Say again,' Flight said urgently. 'Paki with the carrier, do you make him?'

Now as chance had it, it was O'Dowd who was now looking towards the building society, and Hood who was facing the wrong way. They heard him say, 'Guvnor says, Paki with the carrier bag: does it contain equipment?' There was a brief pause and O'Dowd's voice, indistinct, before Hood came back clearly. 'Says

14

it's nearly empty, but definitely something in there. Query small firearm.'

'Right,' Flight said. 'He's our man, okay? So listen: Chitty and me, we'll go to the car now. When he comes out, you follow; and if he runs, don't you run till we're well past him. And tell One-Three, will you – opposite pavement preferable.' The Asian man had just paused, right outside the building society door, and they saw him glance around one last time before going inside. Flight looked to Chitty. 'Let's go,' he said.

Getting out of the junk shop downstairs proved unexpectedly problematical. A high-sided van had pulled up at the kerb and two removal men were manoeuvring an old, upright piano – old enough to have brass candle holders either side of the music-rest – out through the door. The piano's new owner, wearing a suede coat and smoking a small cigar, watched anxiously. When he spoke there was a distinct trace of West Coast American in his voice.

'I searched all over London for one like that; so you just be careful, y'hear?'

The removal men were doubly careful: Flight and Chitty waited, trying not to let their mounting anxiety and urgency show, because the girl serving in the shop was already looking at them, and wondering . . .

'Has he come?' she called.

'It's okay, Miss Eisner,' Flight returned, as reassuringly casual as he could manage. 'We'll be back after lunch.'

The removal man had managed to get the piano on to the pavement now and Flight and Chitty both made a less than casual dive out through the door. Rounding the front of the removal van, Flight was relieved to see O'Dowd and Hood still in place, so the game-plan was still on 'go'. Reaching the squad's unmarked Astra,

Flight unlocked the doors and he and Chitty climbed inside.

'Bit close, wouldn't you say?' Flight was looking towards O'Dowd and fretting. Chitty just shrugged. Flight looked at his watch. 'How long's matey been in there?'

'Four, five minutes.'

'Must be busy,' Flight observed grimly.

From his position twenty feet from the door of the building society, O'Dowd could see that within they *were* busy: queues from all three of the counter positions that were open; at least nine, maybe twelve customers in all. He had lost sight of the suspect now which meant he had either reached the front of his queue, or was very near. So any minute now . . . Behind him, temporarily intruding on his concentration, he could hear the removal men being supervised as they eased the old piano up the ramp towards the back of their van. 'Easy . . . I said, easy! Left! Left! No, not my left – *your* left! For Chrissake! You know what you got there? . . . Okay, now just take it easy . . .'

From within the building society there was a sudden, piercing scream. O'Dowd froze. The scream was followed by another: and then pandemonium. A man came hurtling out through the doors, yelling to all and sundry, 'He's got a gun!! . . .'

O'Dowd wasn't aware of any conscious thought before he moved: he just went, like a reflex reaction, impulse, charging for the doors. Inside the car, Flight saw him go. Grabbing his PR he yelled desperately, 'No! One-Five, tell him! Stop him! . . .' But it was too late. O'Dowd had disappeared inside.

Customers were cringing against the walls, cowering on the floor. A woman was sobbing. Behind the counter no one was in sight. The staff had all hit the deck and were staying below eye level. The man with the gun was backing towards the door as O'Dowd burst through and launched himself upon him. The gunman flailed wildly, twisting and thrashing, lashing out with hands and feet. The butt of his gun caught O'Dowd right in the groin. O'Dowd felt all his breath empty out of his lungs in a single explosion of pain. He released his hold on the bloke and doubled up. Dropping his gun in his panic, the robber turned and fled.

Out on the pavement Hood saw the man emerge and take off up the street. There was something about him . . . and his struggle to place it momentarily interfered with what he should have been doing – which was giving chase. It lost him several vital seconds. By the time he had pulled himself together and had started in pursuit, the man had already reached the first intersection and had disappeared around the corner.

Inside the Astra, Flight rammed the car into gear and lurched out into the traffic; but that was as far as he managed to get because the removal van created a bottle-neck which was blocked solid by oncoming vehicles. In pure frustration Flight bashed his horn two, three, four times; which earned him a V-sign from one of the oncoming drivers, and that was all.

Feet pounding, his insides jarring at each stride, Hood reached the intersection and careered around the corner to a panting halt. He looked along the street; he turned a full three hundred and sixty degrees, desperately scanning *all* of the streets that led off from here like spokes from a hub . . . but there was no running figure; no sign of the gunman at all.

Standing on the ramp behind their van, still holding the piano, the removal men were gaping at the scene: Flight emerging from the Astra and O'Dowd, still somewhat stooped, groping out from the building society.

'O'Dowd . . !' Flight shouted.

'Sorry, guv,' O'Dowd managed back. 'Bastard got me in the nuts. Where's Steve?'

'Nicking him. We hope!'

'It's alright, he'll be okay,' O'Dowd said. 'Fella dropped his gun. It's in there.' He gestured vaguely back to the building society.

'In there,' Flight repeated in some incredulity. 'So what are you doing out here, O'Dowd?! Go back in and GET it!!'

O'Dowd turned back for the doors, still not able to move all that quickly. But then he was saved the trouble, because a youngish bloke, one of the customers, at that moment emerged, bearing the gun.

''S'alright,' he called. ''S'not real! 'S'just a starting pistol – look!' And he pointed it into the air.

'Sir!' Flight yelled. 'Please put that down! . . .'

But the man was not going to be denied his moment, and he pulled the trigger. The gun shot reverberated between the buildings, even over the noise of the traffic. Instinctively, the two removal men ducked – and jumped. Left to its own devices, the piano started gently backwards, then gathered speed. It hit the road at such a runaway rate not even its owner would have dared try to arrest it. It swayed, tilted, remained poised for a tantalizing moment, and then toppled over with a cacophonous, twanging crash.

3

Detective Chief Inspector Munro turned the pages of the report and read with a deliberation that was, in itself, frighteningly eloquent. Sitting opposite him, O'Dowd could feel the atmosphere becoming heavier and more oppressive by the page. Eventually Munro spoke.

'Mmm. Yes.' He looked up. 'Have you had a copy, O'Dowd?'

'Sir?'

'Your annual qualifying report. Did Inspector Flight give you a copy?'

'Er, yes, Mr Munro. Yes, sir.' And to prove the point O'Dowd hurriedly produced his own copy from his inside pocket. Munro sniffed and returned to his reading. O'Dowd had no wish to read again, for himself, the damning indictments Rockliffe had laid against him; but in the almost unbearable strain of the moment even that was preferable to doing nothing but watch Munro soak it all in. O'Dowd braced himself, and began to read.

After a moment Munro leant across to his intercom and flicked a switch. 'Gilly? No calls for the next – twenty minutes. And bring me in a glass of water, will you?' He leant back and surveyed the uncomfortable O'Dowd. 'Well?'

'Sir?'

'Agree, disagree? Fair, unfair?'

O'Dowd swallowed. He was being given his chance. The question was: did he dare grasp it?

'Strongly disagree, sir. Very unfair.'

Munro sniffed again. From his jacket pocket he took

out a small sachet and squeezed from it a couple of brightly coloured pills. At just about the same moment there was a tap on his door and his secretary entered with the glass of water. As she retreated O'Dowd caught the glance she gave him, but he couldn't work out whether it was sympathetic or condescending. Normally he would have given her a grin because Gilly was worth it and O'Dowd wasn't beyond holding out certain hopes in that direction; but today was decidedly not normal.

He watched Munro take the pills, half turned away from him, fastidious, discreet, and found himself speculating on what they were for. Heart? No, dodgy ticker and he'd be on half pay by now; Force doctor would have insisted. Vitamins?! Maybe Marilyn was a health food freak! Reminded of the nickname Georgiou had come up with for Munro, he couldn't help smiling to himself.

'Doesn't make happy reading, does it?'

With a slight start O'Dowd realized that Munro had returned to the report, and that wiped the smile off his face double quick.

'No, sir.'

'See, O'Dowd – the annual report's where we take a breather. Stand back from the hustle and bustle of the Crime Squad and take a long, cool look at our . . . fledglings. Because that's what you are, O'Dowd. Out of the egg, a uniform PC in mufti; but not yet ready to fly with CID. The Crime Squad's a school, really; a training college; and your books and lessons are the streets of London. Yes?'

O'Dowd concurred. There wasn't much else he could do, while wishing privately that Munro would get on with it and not take him on a walk all round the garden first.

'Where are you from, Gerard? Originally?'

'Liverpool, sir.'

'Ah. Yes, I thought I detected a twang. Liverpool: bolshy bloody lot up there, aren't they?'

In the current circumstances and in the interests of self preservation, O'Dowd wasn't sure whether it was wise to contest that or not. But then, perhaps proving Munro's point, he said, 'All that's just a myth, sir, really.'

'Really.' Munro's tone was dry but not hostile. 'The thing is, Gerard, I'm in an awkward position. New to this job; new to the ground . . . very much the new boy, feeling his way. I don't know you; or Sergeant Rockliffe, not well. Is there some kind of personality clash between you?'

'Not so much a clash, Mr Munro,' O'Dowd replied, the Liverpudlian in him now really showing himself over the parapet, 'more I'm the road and he's the steamroller.'

To his relief, Munro laughed; at least, that's what O'Dowd took it to be, a strange, clipped, bark of a sound. In case he was wrong he kept his own expression studiously impassive.

'Fair enough,' Munro said. 'Yes, he's a prickly customer, your sergeant. Brilliant in his day, so rumour has it. Could have got to the top.' He nodded to himself and then, oddly, as though ruminating, he repeated it. 'To the top.' For a moment Munro seemed to have gone away from O'Dowd entirely, lost in some contemplation that O'Dowd couldn't fathom. But then, abruptly, he collected himself and his voice was suddenly harder and crisper and less ingratiating. 'It says here you're foolhardy and impetuous; prone to rush in where angels fear to tread. I don't see, on the evidence to date, how you can altogether refute that.'

'No sir. Only it's hard, you know? When the adrenalin's going. You see the body, like, and you want the body . . . and that's it.'

'For you, it is, or seems to be, yes.' Which definitely implied criticism.

O'Dowd decided to fight back. Because Rockliffe *had* been unfair; the report *was* unfair, and, having come this far, he didn't see why he shouldn't at least try to set it straight. 'Yeah, only all what's happened recently, everything that's gone wrong, most of it's just been bad luck.'

'Luck? That's loser's talk, O'Dowd.' There was a pause. 'Ambitious?'

'Sir?'

'I'm asking whether you're ambitious.'

'Yes, sir. Very.'

'Curb it. Starting today. Don't try and pole-vault when you're still in your nappies, O'Dowd. Got it?'

'Yes, sir.' So the matey-matey bit had been a blind and it was a dressing down after all. O'Dowd hauled down his Liverpudlian colours and sat, stony.

'You've been told you're being taken off the building societies case, I take it?'

'No, sir . . .'

'Well you are. Inspector Flight doesn't want you around, not while there's a risk of firearms. May have only been a starting pistol this time, but you're lucky that's all it was! And so are those customers you might have been putting at risk! We can't afford to have you running amok again, O'Dowd, because next time God knows what he'll bring. Okay?'

'It'll have to be, won't it, sir?' O'Dowd replied stonily.

4

If O'Dowd was unhappy about being removed from the building society investigation, Janice Hargreaves was positively distraught. Because the ramifications were that Adams would replace O'Dowd, and O'Dowd would replace Adams; which meant that O'Dowd would now be working with her and she, quite simply, didn't like him.

Why? He wasn't racist; not like Steve Hood was racist. Steve Hood had actually made it clear he wouldn't work with her under any circumstances and that had been a very ugly few days. O'Dowd wasn't bad-looking, either; nor did he smell, nor did he seem to have any intolerably unpleasant personal habits . . . but what he did have was an ego the size of an airship and an outrageously overwhelming belief in his irresistibility to women! And the fact that she had gone out of her way to disabuse him, rather than deflating him in the slightest, had only seemed to make him more determined to prove his point. Working together was going to be intolerable! But if it was, if that's how it proved to be – really, really intolerable – well, she did have one secret weapon in her armoury that would cut just about any man down to size. That's if Keith Chitty was to be believed, because it was he who had told her; it was he who had been with O'Dowd in the changing rooms that day, and it was he whose objective opinion an anxious O'Dowd had sought, concerning the size, no less, of his manhood. And in all objective honesty, Chitty told her, he had had to say that it was perhaps just a little – just slightly – abnormal in its diminutive, if passive, state.

'What a put-down,' she thought. 'You come on strong with me, O'Dowd and I'll prick your ego so bad you won't ever dare blow it up again!'

As it turned out, Munro had already done enough of a demolition job on O'Dowd's ego for her to have no trouble, not, at least, on their first time out together. If anything O'Dowd was withdrawn and very docile, almost sullen. Privately Hargreaves had to admit to herself that he wasn't at all bad looking; but it was a face that could look spoilt and petulant and that was the way he was looking now, self-pitying. Janice had no time for it so, for the most part, they drove in silence.

Their call was to a woman with an Arab-sounding name who had reported, on three occasions now, the presence of what was probably a Peeping Tom outside her house. Peeping Toms were unpleasant, but not dangerous, providing they stayed just Peeping Toms. The trouble was there was no guaranteeing they wouldn't graduate to something worse and, in her case, the persistence of the man's nocturnal visits warranted in Rockliffe's eyes a determined stake-out to catch him.

It was a quiet street of tree-lined, Regency houses, all in immaculate repair. It positively smelt of money. The house numbers were difficult to decipher from the road so Janice parked the car in the first available space and they climbed out. A few yards further down a man was clipping his hedge with electric shears and O'Dowd ambled towards him.

"Scuse me, John.'

'Yes?'

'We're looking for number fifteen.'

'Oh yes? Who did you want there?'

O'Dowd was about to reply that that wasn't any of his business, but then Janice joined them and said simply, 'A Miss Soom . . . Souhami . . .'

'Sonia?'

'Yeah.' O'Dowd nodded.

The man pointed to the next-door gate. 'Nearly right,' he said.

O'Dowd gave him an insolent smirk in acknowledgement and moved on towards the gate.

'Are you the caterers?' the man called after them.

'Nosey bloody Parker,' O'Dowd thought. 'No, John,' he said. 'We're the bomb disposal experts.'

The man returned to his hedge clipping with an expression of disdain and O'Dowd smiled to himself, feeling that maybe he was beginning to get back into his stride again.

There was an answerphone buzzer at the door of number fifteen which O'Dowd pressed, and they waited. As they did so their eyes ranged over the well-kept garden, the driveway and the garage. O'Dowd's eyes, in particular, lingered on the Ferrari and the Mercedes, both spotless, neither more than a couple of years old, which stood parked in front of the garage doors. He became aware that Janice was regarding him, and there was that certain look in her eye. She had very expressive eyes, did Janice Hargreaves, very knowing, in an amused kind of way. Forestalling her, he said, 'What? Jealous? Who? – Me?!'

But those knowing eyes weren't going to be taken in by that attempted disclaimer. She pursed her lips sceptically, and looked away. 'Just don't forget to wipe your feet when we get in, okay?'

From the box on the wall a voice suddenly addressed them. 'Yes?'

'PC O'Dowd and WPC Hargreaves, Crime Squad,' O'Dowd offered back. The door buzzer grated and they pushed inside.

The interior of the house was clearly going to be no disappointment, entirely in keeping with the two cars parked outside. Everything smacked of money and plenty of it, though not in any garish or overly osten-tatious way. A broad Persian carpet stretched the length of the hall. The light fittings were modern chandeliers, clusters of crystal pear-drops around brass candle-bulb holders. The pictures on the walls were all originals, abstracts, and even if O'Dowd didn't know the artist he'd have been willing to bet that Dave Adams would. Because Adams came from that kind of background and knew about these things, art, theatre, music; and whoever had painted these pictures, O'Dowd would have been equally willing to bet, wasn't just some nobody.

'Think she takes in lodgers?' he muttered to Janice. But before she could respond they were aware of a figure descending the stairs, skipping almost, down towards them.

'Miss Souhami?' Janice asked.

'Hello,' the girl said.

She could have been anything between seventeen and twenty-nine. She was pale, olive brown with bare feet, bare legs, and wide brown eyes. Her hair was long, tousled, raven black. For a moment O'Dowd just gawped. She was the good life; straight out of one of those TV ads where the people were all impossibly beautiful. She was smiling at them, and her teeth were another ad all on their own. Suddenly he realized that she was waiting, as was Janice, and he felt himself starting to go red. 'Oh ta, thanks a bunch,' he thought.

He coughed awkwardly. 'Yeah, well . . . we've got an appointment with – well is it your big sister or something? Miss Sonia Souhami?'

The girl smiled again. 'I'm as big as they grow in my family, I'm afraid. Come on through, why not?' She started to lead the way down the hall. 'We may as well sit in the conservatory. It overlooks the garden. Sorry about all the mess.'

O'Dowd glanced at Janice: *mess*?! . . . Janice just raised her eyebrows and let her eyes say it all.

The conservatory, not unexpectedly, was light and sunny and softly perfumed with the scent from a number of exotic blooms which neither O'Dowd nor Janice had ever seen before. One wall was entirely glass, giving on to a small, private rear garden, mostly grass, beyond which could be seen the garden square belonging to all the residents around it who cared to join and contribute to its upkeep. Between Sonia's garden wall and the railings of the square there was a quiet access road, used mostly for parking. It was a tranquil scene; quiet, verdant, restful; but Janice was trying to imagine what it would be like at night: pretty dark, that's for sure, with plenty of cover for the creeping prowler.

'I've made some tea,' Sonia announced, rejoining them with a couple of extra cups and saucers. The teapot was already on the table. 'You'll join me?' Neither needed to be asked twice. Sonia laughed. 'I always imagine policemen drinking a lot of tea. O'Dowd's an Irish name, though, isn't it?'

'Got it in one.'

'But you're not Irish.'

'No, er – Liverpool Irish.'

Sonia nodded and poured. 'I'd like to visit Ireland. My father owns a factory in County . . .' It had escaped her. 'Oh, County Something. Kerry? Killarney?'

O'Dowd's knowledge of the land of his ancestors was sketchy, to say the least. He shook his head, unable to help her, while half resenting and half envying the casual carelessness she displayed over one of the sources of her wealth. 'Must be nice,' he thought, 'to have that much you can afford to forget where the odd factory is.' 'Great place,' he said, 'this,' indicating the house.

Sonia had settled in a swing seat and was gently

pushing herself backwards and forwards with those bare toes. 'Oh, d'you like it? Yes, nice little house really. Cosy.' She smiled at him and he was transfixed by her: those bare feet and bare legs as the seat lazily turned and swung. 'I bought it two years ago but I'm not sure how long I'll keep it. I'm rather . . .' She shrugged. '. . . fidgety, I suppose.'

'Are you?' O'Dowd said. Sonia nodded. This time, they both smiled.

Janice was beginning to feel distinctly like a gooseberry. She could see what was going on and, quite frankly, it had stopped being amusing and had started to become a bore. If O'Dowd wanted to dabble in these sorts of waters where, any instant, he was likely to find himself out of his depth, well that was his business. And if he was prepared to let himself be suckered by teasing young ladies like Sonia Souhami, well that was his business as well; but it wasn't what they were here for.

'So, about this man,' she said abruptly, cutting in on their private eyeballing. 'Would you like to tell us about him?'

Sonia, very unfazed, turned towards her. 'Yes. The man. The first time I saw him was about a fortnight ago. I was in here, watering the plants. It was . . . well, certainly late at night. I looked up, and there he was. Just there.'

'At the glass?' Janice asked.

'No, standing in the middle of the garden. Not moving or anything. Just standing. With something over his face.'

'A mask?' O'Dowd said, deciding that he had better start being a bit professional as well.

'Not exactly . . .'

'A balaclava, then?'

'A what? . . . Oh, yes – those woolly hats: yes, it could have been. I went to the french windows there,

28

opened them and said, "Who are you? What are you doing?" And he . . . well, he just turned and ran. Jumped over the wall and off into the square.'

'Did he . . . expose himself?' Janice asked. 'Anything like that?'

'Not so that I could see. Mind you, I wasn't looking very hard.' She gave a small laugh. 'Then, a few days later, he was back again. Same thing: just standing, not moving. But then, last weekend, I was having a bath. The bathroom's on the first floor with a little balcony. And there he was, on the balcony, looking in. I suppose he must have climbed up the drainpipe?' She looked between them as though wanting their confirmation of this assumption, but they didn't respond. 'Anyway, this time it was me who ran – out of the bathroom to dial nine-nine-nine!'

Janice nodded. 'I see. What's the easiest way into the garden square?'

'Through the gate over there, I suppose.'

'Do you mind if I have a look around the garden?'

'No, of course . . .' Sonia rose and opened the french windows for her. Janice stepped outside and began, slowly, to cross the lawn, looking for footprints or maybe something the prowler might have dropped. Sonia turned back to O'Dowd. 'So what will you do?'

'Probably mount an observation for a few nights.'

'What? In here?'

'No, outside. But tucked away, like. We've got ways of doing it.'

'I see. Sounds intriguing.'

For a brief moment O'Dowd was tempted to play up to that; make the job sound glamorous and exciting and dangerous, even. But then he realized how difficult, once started, it would be to maintain, given that the truth was so completely the opposite. Besides which, he wasn't at all sure that Sonia wasn't a lot more knowledgeable and worldly-wise than she pretended, and the thought of making himself appear ridiculous in her eyes was simply unbearable.

He shook his head. 'No, it's not. Mostly it's just dead boring. And cold.'

'Poor you!' said young Miss Sonia Souhami.

And the way she said it left O'Dowd in no doubt at all. She was definitely interested. More than interested! She was practically begging for it! But he'd never been involved with a bird like this one before, living the sort of life she must lead, used to that much money. It left him floundering. And at a loss. What the hell was she interested in *him* for? God's gift to women he may be, but a bird like this? . . . Maybe she wasn't interested at all; maybe she was just playing a game, amusing herself at his expense . . . The pause between them widened.

O'Dowd looked out to the garden and saw that Janice had disappeared through the gate into the square. No help coming from that quarter! The pause between them was becoming embarrassing.

In desperation, O'Dowd gave up the high-wire juggling and jumped for the safety net of what he was and why he was here: a copper, doing his job.

'Does anyone else live here?' he asked.

She shook her head. 'No one. Not even domestic staff, that's its charm for me. London's the only place where I can be completely alone. If I want.'

'There she goes again,' O'Dowd thought, 'another invitation.' She seemed to be leaving the door open so damn wide, he couldn't understand why he didn't just walk through it. But still he didn't; partly because he was too scared – though he would never have admitted as much, even to himself – and partly because an idea had just occurred to him which he genuinely felt worth pursuing.

'Er, your father, has he got any enemies?'

'Everyone in the Gulf's got enemies. Why do you ask that?'

'Dunno really.' O'Dowd paused for effect. He didn't want his idea to go cheap. 'It's just, this feller, he may be a flasher, yeah, sure . . . But he could be somebody else, couldn't he?'

'Somebody else? . . .'

'Somebody who's got it in for you or your Dad.'

There was a brief pause, and then she laughed, as though the notion was absurd. 'Nobody knows I live here. I've made sure of that.'

'Look, if they want you, they'll find you,' O'Dowd countered, warming to his theory. 'No question. And here you are, all alone, no protection, no bodyguards . . .'

He had the impression that she might now have decided to take him seriously because her face had become pensive and flat. 'I've had bodyguards all my life,' she said quietly. 'Even at prep school. Pa always made sure there was someone patrolling the grounds. Discreetly, of course, so as not to upset the other girls. But not now. No. Now I decide. For myself. Now I live on my own terms.'

And as her eyes came up to meet O'Dowd's it was as though there was a challenge in the way they flashed: daring him to contest her right to do so.

5

The answer came to Hood when he was in the canteen, half way through his lunch. It had been bothering him on and off for two days and now there it was, out of nowhere! So sudden, so unexpected, and such a mind-boggling realization that he almost choked on the chicken and ham pie he was chewing.

'I know him . . . !' he wheezed and he gasped for breath. 'Bleedin' Henry, I know him!'

Chitty and Georgiou, with whom he was sharing the table, stared at him in surprise and bewilderment.

'Want a slap on the back?' Chitty offered.

Hood shook his head, grabbed his glass of water and drank deep.

'Know who?' Georgiou asked.

'I was at school with him!' Hood exclaimed and banged his glass down so hard on the table that the rest of the crockery jumped.

'Who?!' Georgiou demanded.

'That building society git! The one who's been knocking over all them building societies!'

Chitty and Georgiou exchanged a look of blank astonishment.

Hood had always known there was something about the man, something familiar, from the first moment of seeing him run out of the building society after O'Dowd had done his lone cavalry charge which had ended so ignominiously. After the man had grappled with O'Dowd, his scarf had fallen from his face so that as he emerged Hood had been able to see him quite clearly. At the time that frisson of recognition had probably cost Hood the collar. But now he didn't just have a face, he had the name to go with it.

'Tarik Azir,' he said, still hardly believing it himself. 'My God, Tarik Azir! We were at school together. I sat next to that geezer for three years!'

'Sat next to him?!' Georgiou said. 'I thought you didn't like Pakis and that?'

'Oh yeah, very funny,' Hood said, and managed not to answer the question.

DI Flight, on hearing the news, was no less astonished, but a good deal more pragmatical. 'Alright,' he said, 'you know him, so you find him. And when you've found him, you lift him!'

'Like a needle in a haystack,' Chitty complained, when Hood roped him in to help.

'Yeah, well you'd know about that,' Hood replied, somewhat unkindly, and thrust Chitty's phone into his hand.

Finding Tarik took them most of the rest of the day.

The address with which they eventually ended up was courtesy of the London Borough of Hammersmith's housing department. But there was some question as to whether it was still current because Tarik Azir, according to their records, hadn't paid any rent for over three months. The final irony on this day of ironies was that the address they were given belonged to a flat on none other than the Dragon Estate.

As they parked the Astra close to the tower blocks they were both reminded of the last time they had been here and the appalling fiasco that had turned out to be. But things like that tended to happen around the Dragon and, as they left the car, it was in both of their minds as to whether it would still be there or still recognizable when they came out again.

The flat was on the third floor. Its next-door neighbour was empty. It had been boarded up at some point but the kids had still managed to get inside and to turn it into something more resembling a demolition site. At least Azir's flat – if it was Azir's flat – still had a door and windows.

'Abandon hope all ye who enter here,' Chitty said somewhat despairingly. Hood knocked at the door. They waited. He knocked again. His patience was beginning to become dangerously stretched when, suddenly, the door opened, maybe an inch; and in the crack they could see a pair of eyes nervously regarding them.

'Yeah?' the voice from within said.

'Tarik?' Hood asked. 'Tarik Azir?'

'Yeah?'

'Come to see you, Tarik. Remember me? Steve Hood? From Woodfell Comprehensive?'

'Eh?' Azir said.

'Come on, Tarik! You sat next to me for years. You can't have forgotten!'

There was a pause. Then, still through that narrow crack, Azir said, 'Who's he?'

'Friend of mine. He's called Keith. I just wanted to see you about something, Tarik. Can we come in?'

There was another brief pause. Then Azir said, 'I'm er . . . bit busy. Yeah. Bit busy, you know? Just now.'

'Only take a minute,' Hood said, smiling reassuringly. 'Honest.' And he pushed on the door, quite gently, but enough to let Azir know that he would have trouble getting it shut again. Reluctantly Azir gave in and turned away, allowing them to enter.

The smell was the first thing that hit them: airless, damp, stale, unhealthy. And then came the state of the place: there was virtually not a stick of furniture in the room: only a few cardboard boxes, an old television, with clothes, old newspapers and bits of crockery scattered everywhere. Hood and Chitty exchanged a glance.

'Yeah, well . . . needs a tidy,' Azir said lamely. It

was difficult to connect him with the figure they had seen outside the building society. Now, when he moved it was a kind of shuffle; he was hunched, his head bowed and gave the impression that everything, talking, moving, just standing, was almost too much effort.

'Moving house or something?' Hood asked.

'No . . .'

'So what's happened to the family, Tarik?'

'Moved north. Leeds. Couple of years ago.'

'Thriving?'

Tarik shrugged. 'You going to kill me?' he said suddenly. 'That why you're here?'

'Kill you? . . .' Hood echoed in some incredulity.

'Duff me up . . . something.'

'Why should we?'

'Well, you're NF, aren't you? After school. You joined, didn't you? The Front. That's what I heard.'

There was a small pause. Hood was aware that Chitty was looking at him. He gave a slight laugh that wasn't as solid and convincing as it should have been. 'Not me, mate. Must've heard wrong. Not a political animal me; never was, never will be.'

'Oh,' Azir said, and didn't seem either relieved or otherwise. The impression he gave was almost one of indifference. He snuffled, like a man who had a bad cold. 'Gotta cigarette? Dying for a smoke. Haven't had a chance to get out today.'

Chitty took out his cigarettes and offered him one. Azir took it and as he accepted a light his fingers were noticeably shaking. 'Thanks.'

'My pleasure,' Chitty said.

Azir pulled on the cigarette deeply, using up a quarter of it in just one drag, head still bowed, shoulders still hunched, refusing to look at either of them.

'Thing is, we're the police, you see, Tarik,' Hood said flatly.

'Who is?' It wasn't fear in his voice so much as surprise.

Hood nodded to Chitty. 'Me and him. That's what I did after I left school. Well, eventually. I joined the Met. I'm in the local Crime Squad. So's Keith.' Azir's eyes now flicked nervously between them. 'And why we're here, we're nicking you, see?'

'What for?' It should have been outraged, indignant even; but it wasn't, it was just flat curiosity.

'Armed robbery. All them building societies you've been doing.'

'Oh,' Azir said again. Chitty began to wonder whether Azir was really comprehending what was going on. Nobody could be *that* disinterested or casual about being arrested . . .

'You do not have to say anything,' Hood was intoning, 'unless you wish to do so, but what you say may be given in evidence.'

Azir said nothing. He just sat down on one of the cardboard boxes and took another long pull on the cigarette.

'That one the bedroom, Tarik?' Hood asked, nodding to a half-open door. It was almost a rhetorical question because they could quite clearly see what appeared to be a mattress with a sleeping bag on top of it lying on the floor. Azir gave a little nod and Chitty went to look.

'Yeah,' Hood continued in a conversational sort of way. 'It was me chased you down the street, Wednesday. Fount Street. After you did the branch there. Didn't even know it was you, not then.'

'I was in Leeds Wednesday.' It was Azir's only attempt at a defence or alibi, but lacked any kind of conviction. The way it came out it was like a token gesture; or perhaps nothing more than just something to say.

'Course you were, son,' Hood replied easily. Azir

snuffled again and wiped his nose on his sleeve. 'Got a cold or something?' Hood asked, though he was pretty sure he knew what the real answer was.

'Dunno.'

'There's something funny about your eyes, too, ain't there?'

'How d'you mean? . . .'

'Something funny about them . . .'

'Steve . . .' Chitty was emerging from the bedroom. In his hand he was holding a hypodermic syringe. Hood nodded slowly. They'd been right all along. A smack-head, maintaining his habit.

'What happened, Tarik?' he said flatly. 'I don't understand it. I mean, at school, you was always dead keen on science, weren't you? Always first with your hand up. Neat handwriting. All the different coloured pens you used. Used to be a pleasure to copy from you. So what happened, eh?'

There was a pause. Azir wiped his nose again, took another drag on the cigarette. Then, without looking at Hood, he said, 'People like you happened.'

Chitty glanced to Hood and caught the look on his face; and it made him wonder what might have happened if he hadn't been there.

It is one of the anomalies of London that its character can vary enormously, ranging from the poorest and the meanest to the richest and most opulent within a relatively very small area. To take a case in point, from the Dragon Estate to the road in which Sonia Souhami lived was, as the crow flies, barely a mile. In reality, it was a world away; a lifetime of dreams away; a different planet.

The unmarked police Transit was parked, as unobtrusively as possible, on the service road at the back of Sonia's garden. Inside, behind the partition which separated the driver's cab from the rear, Janice and

O'Dowd were having to come to terms with their enforced intimacy. Stake-outs were bad enough, just sitting, waiting, watching, hoping, not knowing how many times it might have to be repeated or whether at the end of it all there would be any positive result to show for it all: so that strained personal relations on top were definitely something you could do without, particularly if there were only two of you.

They had been there for two hours now and so far, Janice had to admit, they weren't doing too badly. In fact O'Dowd on his own, when he wasn't feeling the need to score points left right and centre and to impress all the others with his wit and prowess, could actually be quite endearing.

He had just finished expounding his theory regarding the flasher, and Janice couldn't help laughing.

'Gerroff,' he said, 'I'm serious. You know, one of them Shite Muslims.'

'One of them what?! . . .' her laughter redoubled.

'Hey, keep it down, will you?' he said anxiously. 'You'll scare him off!'

'*Shi'ite*, you wally!'

'Yeah, well – one of them. Probably wants to hold her to ransom. Like Patti Hearst.'

'Say this for you, O'Dowd,' Janice conceded, 'you haven't half got a terrific imagination.' She reached for her thermos and gingerly, in the darkness, poured herself a mug of liquid.

'What's that?'

'Diet soup. Tomato. I think it's tomato. Want some?'

O'Dowd declined rather emphatically. He glanced at his watch. Just gone midnight. They'd give it another half hour, maybe, and if nothing had turned up by then . . .

Through his headset he suddenly heard Control calling them. As he took the message his voice began to grow tense.

'What?' Janice asked.

'Sonia Souhami's just been on to the station; she's heard noises. Reckons there might be somebody on her balcony again.'

'If there is,' Janice said, shocked, 'he hasn't come past us.'

'Better check it out,' O'Dowd said. 'You hang on here. I'll call if there is anybody.' He opened the back door. 'You be alright?' he asked, which Janice found quite touching.

'Yeah,' she said. 'Go on.'

O'Dowd clambered out and softly closed the door.

Practically as soon as he was in the garden it was abundantly clear to him that there was nobody on Sonia Souhami's balcony. But in the open french windows of the conservatory, waiting for him, there *was* Sonia Souhami. She was cradling a sleek Persian cat and looked somewhat abashed.

'I'm sorry,' she said. 'False alarm, I'm afraid. It was just Soloman wanting to be let in.'

Soloman, O'Dowd took it, was the cat. 'No harm done,' he said. 'Best to be on the safe side.' And that should have been that. He should have turned and headed straight back to the van but, for some reason, he didn't.

'Will you come in for a minute?' she said.

'What for?' he asked.

'There's something I'd like to talk to you about.'

'Yeah, but . . . I shouldn't be away from the van, see?'

'Not even for a minute?'

'Yeah, well, mustn't be any longer.' He was beginning to wonder whether Soloman had even been out of the house, let alone on the balcony that night. Pedigree cats like that weren't usually let out on the tiles.

39

'Don't look so worried,' Sonia said. 'If he was coming tonight he'd have been by now, anyway.'

She led him inside, through the conservatory and into a drawing room, which simply took his breath away. Involuntarily he gave a whistle.

'Nice, isn't it?' she said.

'Not bad, for a broom cupboard.'

'Would you like a drink?'

'Hey no, look, I said only a minute and I meant it.'

'Gin? Vodka? Scotch?'

Christ, was she persistent, he thought and shook his head.

'Irish?'

Irish! If O'Dowd had a weakness for booze, that was it. But rather than admit defeat he said, 'What was it you wanted to talk about?'

Sonia smiled and crossed to the drinks cabinet. 'I've been thinking about what you were saying.'

'What was I saying?'

'About security. Personal security. I want to put a proposition to you. I'd like you to be my bodyguard.'

Now, it is true that O'Dowd had heard of these things happening, but until that instant he had never actually *believed* that they happened. Oh sure, coppers retired after their twenty years or twenty-five and picked up lucrative security jobs in hotels or big firms, that was routine. But to be personal bodyguard to a dark-skinned, walking dream! . . . He felt like pinching himself to make sure that wasn't what he was doing – dreaming.

'Water? Soda?' Sonia asked.

'Er – yeah . . . No – neat. Please.'

She brought him his drink and indicated the long sofa. As they sat, he noticed that her feet and legs were bare once again.

'What's your first name, by the way? I'd rather not go on calling you O'Dowd.'

'Gerry. Gerard.' He was beginning to persuade himself that this *wasn't* a dream. There was usually no sense of taste in dreams, and this Irish was tasting the best he had ever known.

'So what do you say?'

'Well, er . . . it's very nice of you . . .'

'You can call me Sonia,' she interjected.

'Very nice of you . . . Sonia. But, I mean, I know it might not show much, but I've got a job already.'

She shrugged. 'How much do you earn?' Nothing if not direct, this little lady!

'Well, er . . . Cheers, by the way . . . About, er – yes, it's about twelve thousand. Sixteen with overtime. Not bad, really.'

Sonia wasn't impressed. 'I have friends who lose more than that in five minutes at a roulette table.'

'So?' He felt put down and belittled and he didn't care for that.

'So, name your price. Obviously you'd have to travel extensively but I always go first class so that wouldn't be too much of a pain.'

'No . . . well right, yeah.' For a moment he struggled. He knew he wasn't dreaming and she really had made the offer, so why did he still not believe it? Things like this just didn't happen to rookie coppers like him! That's why! 'You're serious, aren't you?' he said.

'Absolutely serious. And what I want, I tend to get.'

He could believe that alright! She rose and walked around to a compact disc player beside which, neatly racked, were a good two yards of discs.

'What kind of music do you like, Gerry?' she asked.

Janice had held out as long as she could, but now she couldn't hold out any longer and, sitting on the portaloo in the back of the van, she was just praying that O'Dowd didn't suddenly return and catch her with her knickers down. What the hell was he doing, anyway?! He should have been back half an hour ago! Well . . . ten minutes, anyway. It certainly didn't take *this* long to check out a balcony. She was even beginning to get slightly worried, but just at this instant the bliss at relieving herself outweighed everything. She started to rise to pull up her jeans, but then she froze: because the light from a torch was suddenly shining through the front windows of the van.

'O'Dowd,' she whispered. But then she remembered that he hadn't taken the torch with him; so whoever this was, it wasn't O'Dowd.

The torchlight snapped off. Holding her breath she thought she could make out light footsteps down the side of the van and, sure enough, a moment later the light was back again, this time shining in from the rear, right over her shoulder. Janice, literally, didn't move a muscle . . . until the light was switched off again and she could hear the footsteps moving away from the van.

Softly Janice moved to the observation window, and was in time to catch the dark shape of a figure opening Sonia Souhami's garden gate and passing through; hardly more than a trick of the night, but she hadn't been mistaken, and that torch had been real enough. She picked up the PR and began to call O'Dowd.

She called him three times, and each time all she got in return was the crackle of static. Her partner's set was obviously switched off. Gritting her teeth and closing her eyes she made herself, and him, a vow: 'I'll murder you for this, O'Dowd,' she said. Then, gently, gently so as to make no noise, she opened the door of the van and eased herself out.

The garden gate was still ajar and coming from the house she could faintly hear the sound of music: something she recognized, Paul McCartney and Wings.

'My Christ, he's gone partying,' she thought, 'leaving me on my own to . . .'

Against the wall of the house a shadow moved. Indistinct at this distance, it mounted a dustbin and then, slowly, began to climb a drainpipe. Janice started towards it at a run.

'Oi! You!' she shouted. 'Stop right there! Police!'

Startled, the figure lost his grip on the drainpipe and fell back on to the dustbin, knocking off the lid, and from thence on to the path. It seemed to Janice that the clatter was sufficient to rouse the whole street but, from within the house, the music continued uninterrupted. She launched herself upon the sprawling, winded figure and grabbed him by his ankles.

'Gerry!' she yelled. 'Gerry!! *Gerry*!!!'

How long she had been calling him before he heard her O'Dowd had no way of knowing. All he caught, dimly through the music, was the sound of his name being screamed from the garden. 'Oh God,' he said, guilt and panic coursing through him like fire.

In the few seconds it took him to reach the conservatory french windows he had imagined every worst possible outcome: the flasher escaped? Janice hurt? Janice *dead*? . . . and his sweat was literally stinging his scalp as he hurtled out on to the path. The sight, in fact, which greeted him was of Janice completely in control holding a darkly dressed and hooded figure in a secure arm lock and pushing him towards the conservatory door. O'Dowd rushed forward to seize the man's other arm.

'Okay, Jan, I've got him,' he panted.

'*You've* got him?!' she cried. 'You mean I've got him, you great Scouse layabout!'

Together they frogmarched the man inside.

'Okay, pal, let's have a look at you,' O'Dowd said, and pulled off the figure's balaclava.

'Well I never,' said Sonia from the doorway. 'It's Edgar Whitney. My next door neighbour.'

'So it is,' said O'Dowd with grim relish.

The man they had met trimming his hedge regarded Sonia with sorrowful, remorseful, adoring eyes.

6

While Hood, Chitty and Hargreaves all earned verbal gongs from DI Flight for their endeavours, O'Dowd picked up nothing but censure. He knew it was deserved, but after the battering he had had that week, one way and another, it somehow didn't seem fair. If anything, it confirmed in him the nagging, growing belief that he and Crime Squads were not exactly made for each other. Oh, he was a good copper, he had no doubts about that. He could be a good detective, too – bloody good! But the way this outfit was run, the stuff they gave you to sort and the way everything had to be done by the book – no room for personal initiative or flair – it just wasn't him. He felt cramped, undervalued, unjustly stigmatized.

There was someone, however, who had recognized him for his true worth: Sonia Souhami. Whether it was his true worth as a bodyguard or as a potential lover, he didn't much care; she wanted him! When he thought of it he still found it difficult to believe (he still had that much humility) but he no longer questioned whether it was for real. It was; she had said so. And all he had to do was decide.

DI Flight as good as made the decision for him; pushing him into her arms, he was, if he only but knew it. In a perverse way O'Dowd almost enjoyed the dressing-down Flight gave him because, tucked away, he had his little secret – not so little either! – his passport out of here, the thing that would render Flight, Rockliffe, the whole damn lot of them entirely irrelevant. The fact that the passport was stamped only one way had actually occurred to him: but this was a scenario of as yet unknown, limitless opportunities. Who could say what might develop from this one lucky break? It was a different world, with a different class of people altogether, with different needs, but needs – he had no doubt – that would always include the likes of himself. And on top of it all, he simply could not dismiss from his mind's eye those bare legs and bare toes, belonging to Sonia Souhami.

The trouble with a good secret, of course, is that nobody knows you've got it, and it is arguable that a secret only really accrues value when it is shared. That was certainly true in O'Dowd's case: there were all the others thinking him a wally, and all the time he had his secret tucked up safe. But the satisfaction that gave him was soon superseded by a need for the others to know. Ridicule him they might, especially Hood and Georgiou; but, deep down, how could they fail to be impressed? The only question was: who to tell? Who could he trust to pass it on, undistorted, unblemished, intact? He chose Dave Adams; because he, of all of them, came from a background that was closer to the world O'Dowd intended to enter than O'Dowd did himself and ought, therefore, at least to understand if not also advise.

Adams received the news with a kind of amused disbelief. 'You're joking . . . ?'

O'Dowd shook his head seriously. 'Straight up. I mean, I know it sounds a bit – you know? But that's what she said: "Name your price". Those were her very words, no kidding.'

'Bloody hell,' Adams said with a soft whistle.

'So what d'you think? I was wondering about thirty grand, something like that. I mean, she's loaded, you know? I mean – *loaded*. What we earn's just beer money to her. So what would you say, eh?'

'What about?'

46

'I'm asking, d'you think thirty thousand's over the top?' O'Dowd repeated impatiently.

'I'd go for fifty,' Adams counselled. 'Nice round sum.'

'Seriously?!' O'Dowd had trouble keeping his voice down.

'Well . . .' Adams said, 'what price do you put on your body, Gerry?' And he laughed.

'Oh great,' O'Dowd returned. 'I thought you might be some help.'

'You're not seriously thinking of taking her up on it though, are you?' Adams said in apparently genuine surprise.

'Why not?!'

'What? Become some rich girl's poodle? I'm surprised at you, Gerry.'

'Well there's not a right lot worth sticking round here for, is there?' O'Dowd returned vehemently. 'Flight and Rockliffe've made that pretty plain. Not much future for me here. So why not? I wouldn't shed any tears leaving this outfit, I tell you.'

O'Dowd's bitterness and seriousness finally got through to Adams. 'So when are you seeing her?' he asked.

'Dunno. Thought I might pop over this evening, actually. You know, just drop in, casual sort of.'

And, though, in fact, the idea had only just presented itself, it suddenly seemed like the only thing to do.

The Ferrari and the Mercedes were still outside the garage, looking as though they hadn't ever moved, as he approached the front door. He took cheer from the sight of them: chances were he would find Sonia at home. He pressed the buzzer. As he waited he quickly ran his fingers through his hair and brushed any dandruff from his shoulders. He was tense, he couldn't deny it, despite the fact he kept telling himself he had no need to be. After all, it was she who had made all the running; it was she who had chosen him. He had been chosen! And what was it she had said? 'What I want I tend to get'? 'Here I am, darling,' he thought, 'all yours.'

He pressed the buzzer again. Something about the silence of the house was beginning to suggest that he might be out of luck after all, that she wasn't at home. But then, instead of the answerphone working, the door itself suddenly opened and there stood a bloke, in his thirties, bearded, with what is usually described as a 'Latin' sort of face. 'Yes?' he said.

It took O'Dowd a moment to recover from the surprise. For some irrational reason he had simply assumed that Sonia would be on her own.

'Oh . . .' he said. 'Er, come to see Sonia.'

'Who are you?' asked the man.

'Friend of the family,' said O'Dowd, beginning to resent the man's manner. 'Why?'

The man just regarded him for a beat. 'She's busy right now.'

'Doing what, John?'

'Mind your own goddam business,' the man said and started to close the door on him.

'Here, steady on, John,' O'Dowd said, getting his foot in the door. 'Don't take that tone with me. I'm a police officer, see?' And he held up his warrant card in front of the man's face. 'PC O'Dowd. Divisional Crime Squad. Case you can't read.'

'Yes, well. That to you, pig-face,' and he raised two fingers in a V-sign. 'Now get your foot out of the door or I'll break it.'

O'Dowd had had enough. He shouldered the door back open wide. 'Got her tied up, have you? While you strip the gaff or something? That what's going on?' And he pushed, violently, past the man and headed down the hallway. The push caused the man to hit his head on the wall and he gave a grunt of pain, but O'Dowd ignored him. Something was going on here, he was sure of it! Sonia wasn't in the conservatory; she wasn't in the drawing room. He tried a third door, entering fast and flattening himself against the wall. As he took in the scene which greeted him he began to feel unspeakably foolish.

'Oh, er . . .'

Seated around a candle-lit dinner table were five – no, six guests, with Sonia at the head. They were in the middle of what looked like a starter course with the white wine in their glasses reflecting and refracting the light of the candles. Most of the guests had looked up at his entrance and now one of the girls giggled.

'Y'okay, Sonia? . . .'

She rose and moved towards him. 'Everybody, this is Gerry, my pet policeman.' She took him by the arm. 'Now what are you doing?' She was smiling but he didn't feel, somehow, that she was really all that amused. 'Charging in like this?' She led him back out into the hallway and shut the door.

'I'm sorry, Sonia,' he said, 'only, see, I thought . . .'

'Don't,' she said, not allowing him to finish. 'Don't ever think. Thinking's not good for some people.'

The man who had opened the door to O'Dowd came up the hallway towards them. He was rubbing his head with his hand. 'Sonia?'

She turned towards him. 'Pedro! . . .'

'He hurt me, Sonia . . .'

'I never!' O'Dowd exclaimed. 'He slipped, that's all.' Sonia was looking back at O'Dowd and she wasn't smiling any more.

'Anyway,' he said to Pedro, 'sorry, pal, sorry.'

'He really hurt me,' Pedro whined.

'He got a bit lippy, see?' O'Dowd appealed to her. 'I mean, like, if he'd just said . . .'

'Get out,' Sonia said quietly.

49

'No, look . . .' O'Dowd persisted.

'Get out!' she said again. And this time there was no question but that she meant for good. So he turned; and he went; with as much nonchalance as he could muster.

And by the time he had got outside the front door he was telling himself what a lucky break he'd had; what a narrow escape; bloody shrew!

In the pub the next lunchtime he managed to get Adams on his own.

'You tell anybody about – you know, what I was telling you?'

Adams shook his head. 'You asked me not to.'

O'Dowd nodded with relief. He hadn't expected Adams to keep to the promise and, indeed, had been more or less counting on him not doing; but now . . . 'Yeah, well. Just forget about it, eh? 'Cos I've had second thoughts. I mean, you were right. I've been thinking about it, and you were dead right, I can see that now. I wouldn't've fitted in that scene – no way!'

A hand descended heavily on his shoulder. He turned, and found himself confronting none other than Rockliffe, his pipe in his mouth, his eyes narrowed in their customary, quizzical squint. Ordinarily it wouldn't have taken O'Dowd by surprise, but today it did, because Rockliffe was supposed to be off sick; had been all week.

'Hello, Skip,' he said. 'What you doing here? I thought you were supposed to be off sick.'

'That's right,' Rockliffe agreed. 'Not officially due back until tomorrow. Only I heard from a little bird that you've been having a bit of a rough week, O'Dowd. So d'you know what I thought? I thought, I'll go in a day early, and I'll buy him a pint.'

Rockliffe's lighter flared above his pipe. And around his eyes, and around his mouth, O'Dowd could swear there was the ghost of a mocking smile.

7

O'Dowd and Hargreaves were sitting no more than five feet from Mrs Maxwell yet were still having difficulty in hearing what she was saying, not because she was softly spoken but because of the volume of the reggae music coming from the next room.

Mrs Maxwell raised her voice. 'I said, Laurel and Hardy!'

'Laurel and Hardy?' O'Dowd looked blankly to Hargreaves who was taking the notes.

'One fat, one thin!' Mrs Maxwell amplified.

O'Dowd nodded. Hell of a description! 'Got that?' he asked Janice. 'One fat, one thin.' Janice dutifully made a note.

The description – if it could be called such – applied to the couple of cowboys who had come knocking at Mrs Maxwell's door a few days previously and had offered to fix the loose slates on her roof; and who, one hour later, had charged her one hundred and fifty pounds and had departed leaving the roof in a worse state than it was to begin with. Just shoddy workmanship? Or deliberate fraud? Over the last week or two there had been a number of similar complaints on the patch and it was beginning to look distinctly like a case of the latter. Which is why the Crime Squad had become involved: if these cowboys were practising deliberate fraud, that made them con-men; and that made them ideal targets for Rockliffe's Babies.

'Turn that damn row off this minute, you hear me?!!' Mrs Maxwell suddenly screamed at the top of her voice, causing Janice and O'Dowd to start visibly. In the next-door room the music died. A moment or two later Mrs Maxwell's two sons, the perpetrators of the din, slouched into the kitchen. The elder of the two was about eighteen and was puffing on what, to O'Dowd, looked suspiciously like a reefer. He found it difficult to believe that anyone could be that blatant, but one of the things about this job, there were new surprises every day.

Mrs Maxwell was explaining to Janice how friendly and plausible Laurel and Hardy had been. She had also, unlike Janice, clocked O'Dowd's sudden interest in her son. Without pausing in her narrative she suddenly rose from her seat, crossed over to the boy and snatched the cigarette out of his mouth. Before O'Dowd's almost disbelieving eyes she threw it straight out of the window then returned to her seat again, still talking.

'Excuse me,' O'Dowd said. Mrs Maxwell paused. He pointed to her sons. 'Who are they?'

'They my two no-account sons.'

'I think he,' pointing to the elder, 'was smoking pot.'

'No, you're wrong,' she returned in a manner that brooked no argument. 'They useless but good boys.' She turned back to Janice again and resumed her narrative.

O'Dowd eyed the boy; the boy eyed him back. His name was Joseph. He had no reason to like white folk, and even less to like the police. O'Dowd could feel the contempt and the hostility emanating out of him and it was implacable.

'But why did you pay them? . . .' Janice was saying.

''Cos I'm stupid,' Mrs Maxwell told her.

'She was afraid,' Joseph said.

'I was not afraid!' his mother rounded on him. 'It was because I'm stupid, always been stupid. The only sensible thing I done was insuring my husband; like money in the bank the way he drank the rum.'

'Did they have transport?' O'Dowd asked. 'These fellas. Car? Van?'

'Van,' Mrs Maxwell replied. 'Small van. They put their ladders on the top. And it was blue.'

O'Dowd nodded. 'You've told us they were like Laurel and Hardy, but is there nothing else you can remember about them? Colour of hair? Accents? Anything that could help us identify 'em?'

'Yeah,' Joseph said, 'they were white.'

O'Dowd gave him a look that was like saying, 'Thanks a bunch!'

Sensing possible trouble once again, Mrs Maxwell said hurriedly, 'Mr Zimmerman, he see them. They cheated him, too, took his window. He maybe can give you a description.'

'Zimmerman?' Janice said. 'Who's . . .'

'Lives in the basement,' Mrs Maxwell told her. 'Nice man. Quiet man.'

Janice and O'Dowd exchanged a glance and then rose. 'Right, well we'll be in touch, Mrs Maxwell,' O'Dowd said, 'if we come up with anything.'

'Some hope,' Joseph said. 'You're going to do nothing, man. But that's fine. 'Cos we can take care of it ourselves. All you need to do is pick up the pieces.'

'Look, you! . . .' O'Dowd said, rounding on him.

'Please, Mister,' Mrs Maxwell intervened. 'He don't mean it. We don't want no trouble.'

For a moment O'Dowd's response lay in the balance, but then he relaxed again and turned back to the mother. 'Ta for calling us, Mrs Maxwell,' he said. 'Like I say, we'll be in touch.' Then he headed for the door.

Hurriedly Janice gathered together her things to follow him. As she did so, Joseph sauntered towards her and from his shirt pocket he brazenly extracted what could only be a reefer and put it into his mouth.

'Hey, sister,' he said, 'what you doing with him?' – meaning O'Dowd.

Janice, who had – until now – been trying not to notice his antics, regarded him sadly and sighed. 'First,' she said, 'I'm not your sister. And second, you're nicked.'

She took hold of him by the collar and hauled him towards the door. Joseph twisted in her grasp, but Janice was a strong girl. 'I'll put the cuffs on if I have to,' she told him.

'Oh Lord,' his mother said behind them. 'Why I got such stupid boys? 'Cos I'm stupid, that's why. It's my fault!'

'No it isn't, Mrs Maxwell,' Janice called back. 'It's his. And he knows it.'

O'Dowd was already at the car as Janice emerged, hauling the protesting Joseph. 'Possession,' Janice said and opened her free hand to reveal the reefer.

O'Dowd nodded. 'I knew it!' he said. 'Blimey, it's come to something when they do it in front of your eyes.' He took charge of Joseph and manhandled him into the car. 'What d'you reckon?' he asked Janice. 'You be alright with him a minute while I go see this Zimmerman fella?'

Janice regarded the surly Joseph in the back of the car: surly, antagonistic – yes, but not dangerous. She nodded. 'Yeah, sure.' And as she climbed in beside Joseph, 'You and me are going to get along just fine, aren't we? We'll swap stories about police harassment, what d'you say?'

Joseph, it seemed, had nothing to say.

O'Dowd descended the steps into the basement area and the first thing which caught his attention was the window, freshly boarded with plywood. Mrs Maxwell's reference to Laurel and Hardy having taken the window hadn't made a lot of sense, but now that he saw it that was clearly exactly what they had done, window frame and all! He knocked on the door. There were geraniums in tubs on either side and a vine, growing from a trough, against the side of the steps where it would catch the sun. The flagstones were clean and swept. Obviously this Mr Zimmerman was a homely, house-proud type who had managed to create his own tiny patch of tranquillity fifteen feet below the street. He was not, however, over-enthusiastic about opening his door. O'Dowd had to knock three times in all and, when the door finally did open, it was only to the extent of its security chain which, O'Dowd noticed, was unusually thick. Behind it was Mr Zimmerman, small, elderly, glasses with an unmistakably Jewish nose.

'Morning, sir,' O'Dowd said cheerfully. 'PC O'Dowd from Church Street police station.' He raised his warrant card for Zimmerman to see. 'Do you think I could just have a word?'

When Zimmerman spoke his voice still contained strong traces of German. 'What do you want?'

'Well, we're making enquiries, see? About a couple of con-men who say they're builders. Mrs Maxwell upstairs says they did some work for you.' He pointed to the window. 'That, I take it. You got caught an' all.'

'I don't know nothing,' Zimmerman said, and started to close the door.

'Hey, but you did see them? . . .' O'Dowd persisted. 'I mean, you did talk to 'em and that?'

Zimmerman dithered. 'Er . . . maybe.'

'So what can you tell me about them? Be an 'elp if you could describe them for us.'

'My eyes,' Zimmerman said, 'not so good.'

'Yeah, well did you pay them any money?'

'Look,' Zimmerman told him, 'I work nightshift. I must get my sleep.'

And this time, he did close the door.

'Some people,' O'Dowd thought. 'You try and help them . . . !' Shaking his head he turned and mounted the steps back up to the street.

As he climbed into the car, Janice said, 'Well?'

'Dunno,' O'Dowd replied. 'Wouldn't talk to me.'

'Why not?' she asked.

'Dunno!' he said. 'Just wouldn't, that's all.'

Behind him, Joseph sniggered.

Hood was not happy. His on/off mate, Terry, whom he had known since school, and who was the used-car salesman who had recently sold Hood his latest motor, couldn't understand it. As far as he was concerned, here he was trying to do Hood a favour and all Hood could do was have a go at him. Chitty, feeling somewhat uncomfortable, watched from the sidelines.

'You conned me!' Hood exclaimed.

'How?!' Terry's tone was all injured innocence.

'Six hundred and bloody fifty you gave me in part exchange! And now you've got it out there marked up at nine hundred!'

'Yeah, well I've got to make a bit of profit, haven't I?'

'You told me . . .' Hood shouted, but Terry didn't let him finish.

'Steve! Steve! Nobody believes a used-car dealer, you know that! An' if you don't, you oughta! Now, you're happy with the motor I sold you, ain't you?'

Instead of reply Hood just kicked the leg of Terry's desk.

Terry grinned. 'See? Another satisfied customer. I ought to be nominated for a knighthood. Fancy a cuppa?'

'Stuff your cuppa!' Hood returned sulkily.

Terry laughed and proceeded to prod a tea-bag into a mug of water.

'These er . . . these merchants with the car,' Chitty

ventured, thinking it was time they got on to why they were actually here. 'They still coming?'

'Ain't phoned none of the other local traders,' Terry replied, 'so looks like they are.'

'Traders?' Hood said. 'Bloody gangsters, more like.'

'What makes you think it's bent?' Chitty persisted.

'I can smell 'em,' Terry told him. 'You get all sorts in this business, but if someone wants to sell a motor they bring it in; they don't *ask* if I'm interested in a certain make, colour an' year first. I said, bring it over, let's have a butcher's. That was four o'clock. Asked me what time I closed, I told 'em five-thirty. Said they wouldn't get here by then so they'd bring it over this morning. Means they must be selling it out of their own manor, if they can't get somewhere in an hour and a half . . .'

'Regular Sherlock Holmes, aren't you?' Hood said cuttingly.

Terry just laughed again. 'One thing,' he said. 'No offence or nothing, only if they do show,' he nodded to Chitty, 'your mate here, he's a bit big, ain't he? Don't exactly blend in, if you take my meaning.'

Hood did take his meaning, precisely; and, moreover, however grudgingly, had to admit that Terry was right. Put Chitty down in the middle of a cattle auction – no problem; but plant him in front of a used-car lot in West London and somehow it just didn't look right.

Across the road from the lot was a small, greasy café from the windows of which, providing one could see through the grime and condensation, it ought to be possible to keep an eye on what was happening opposite.

'We'll get a cuppa over at Fred's,' Hood said.

'Good idea,' Terry approved. 'You'll have no trouble clocking it when it comes: X-Reg Cortina, blue. There'll be two blokes in it. They always come in

57

twos, don't trust each other.' He grinned. 'Usual idiots, always think they're being conned.'

Hood recognized the reference to himself. 'This better be a good one,' he said threateningly. 'You better not be wasting our time, that's all.'

'Come on,' Chitty said, 'or they'll be here, won't they?'

The café was definitely working men's: formica-topped tables, tin ashtrays, sugar dispensers that delivered a veritable avalanche each time you used one. The ketchup bottles had caked ketchup on them and there were flies in profusion. Hood had retreated inside his copy of *The Sun* leaving Chitty to keep an eye on the street. Half an hour or more had passed and Chitty was uncomfortably aware of the glances that were beginning to be cast in their direction by the café proprietor and his wife. It was coming up towards lunchtime, and they were still occupying a table all for the price of two cups of tea.

He looked out of the window again, and suddenly he saw something which made him nudge Hood's arm.

'What? . . .' Hood followed Chitty's gaze. After a beat he said, 'That's a van; a blue van. That's not a Cortina . . .'

'Yeah, I know,' Chitty agreed. 'Laurel and Hardy – look.'

'Who?! . . .'

'Laurel and Hardy, them blokes Gerry and Janice were talking about this morning – scam builders.'

Hood looked back to the van. It was parked on the hard-standing in front of a house just beyond the used-car lot. Its occupants, one fat and one thin, had got out and while the thin one unroped the ladders from the van's roof-rack, the fat one was talking to the householder, pointing up to the guttering and taking notes in a small book.

'Could be,' Hood admitted.

'Got to be,' Chitty said.

'Well that's charming that is,' Hood complained. 'We nick them we'll blow it for the other.'

'Suppose so,' Chitty agreed glumly. But then he cheered up. 'But they're not going anywhere, are they? Here, you keep obbo a minute, I'll be right back.' And he got up and headed for the serving counter.

The sight of his warrant card didn't do the proprietor's ticker any good at all. Nor did the realization that he had had two coppers sitting in on him for the last three quarters of an hour. But when Chitty explained that all he wanted was the use of the phone the man's pulse rate began to slow down again. Not that he was anything other than a decent, law-abiding café owner; but there were some catering-sized cans of soup, and luncheon meat and suchlike in his storeroom that he had come by via, shall we say, slightly unusual sources – like one of the chefs in the hospital kitchens for instance!

Chitty wasn't long making his call, and he even paid for it, which the proprietor considered pretty decent of him, considering. Returning to Hood, Chitty said, 'They're passing the message.'

Hood nodded. His eyes were fixed on the car lot across the road where, Chitty saw, a blue Cortina containing two youngish men had just pulled on to the forecourt.

'It's all happening, ain't it?' Hood said. 'Come on.'

Terry was sauntering around the car examining it as they approached. The two occupants were standing, hands in pockets, watching him. Chitty took up position on the pavement to block the way if anyone did a runner, while Hood went forward towards the group around the car. Terry saw him coming.

'Alright, Steve?'

Hood turned to the first of the two men. 'This your car, sir?'

'What's it to you?' the man returned.

His mate nudged his arm and nodded back to Chitty who now had his radio out and was passing on the car's details to Control.

'That the paperwork?' Hood asked, pointing to the papers in the bloke's hand. He thought he detected in the second man a sudden readiness to run. 'Don't even think about it, cocker,' he told him. 'My mate'd break your back.'

'Here, what's this all about,' the first man complained, turning on the indignation. 'You think we nicked it?!'

'Course not,' Hood said. 'Keith! . . .' he called.

'Checking,' Chitty called back.

'Go into the office, shall we?' Hood suggested to the two blokes. 'Don't mind, do you, Terry?'

'Be my guest,' Terry said. 'Only hurry it up. Bad for business having the filth all over.'

'Price you pay for being an honest citizen,' Hood told him, and shepherded the two men towards the office building.

Chitty was still waiting for Control to come back on the car's details when the Squad Astra pulled up at the kerb behind him. He turned on hearing his name.

'Got a message on the PR,' O'Dowd said. 'Where are they?'

Chitty just pointed to the blue van beyond the forecourt.

O'Dowd nodded and began to roll the car forward.

Over his PR Chitty heard Control coming back to him. The Cortina had been reported stolen three days previously. He headed after Hood to give him the good news.

Inside the Astra, Janice and O'Dowd could see Laurel and Hardy at work. Laurel was up at the top of the ladder doing something to the guttering, while Hardy was standing at the bottom, presumably to hold the ladder steady, though in fact he seemed more interested in . . . He was looking directly at them.

'We've been clocked!' O'Dowd said. He rammed his foot on to the accelerator and the Astra spurted forward to box in the van. Hardy had already scrambled inside it while Laurel was starting down the ladder. Janice and O'Dowd leapt out of their car and while O'Dowd headed for the van, Janice went to meet Laurel. They arrived at the foot of the ladder at about the same moment. Laurel looked round and saw Janice standing there. There was a brief pause and then he started to climb the ladder again.

'I don't know where you think you're going,' Janice said and she reached out and grabbed hold of him by his belt. Laurel offered no resistance and meekly returned to earth.

Looking in through the van's window O'Dowd came face to face with Hardy. O'Dowd nodded to him. Hardy didn't respond. He was furiously chewing something with a kind of sick expression on his face, and seemed to have difficulty in swallowing. O'Dowd made out what it was he was eating from the scrap that remained in the fat man's hand. It was the tax disc from the van's windscreen. O'Dowd shook his head to himself. 'It's alright,' he called through the glass. 'They do feed you down the nick, you know.'

8

Laurel's name turned out to be Brian; Hardy's real name was Frank – or Francis John William Augustus, to be precise, but he answered mostly to Frank.

The couple of likely lads with the stolen Cortina were called Tommy and Rod.

The sudden influx as they were all brought into the station at the same time had the Custody Sergeant scratching his head as to where to put them all, and a short game of musical interview rooms followed with folk being shunted around, to the cells, to CID, to the seats in reception even, as he tried to accommodate them. One of the bit-players in this pantomime was none other than Joseph Maxwell, whose bail papers had been drawn up and awaited his signature. Not that it was anyone's fault, but it was unfortunate that he was brought into the charge room while Frank and Brian were both still in there. Joseph recognized them instantly.

'That's him!' he shouted. 'That's the pair!'

'What's your problem, mate?' Frank demanded.

'I ain't your mate!' Joseph said viciously, and he lunged for Frank evidently intent on getting his hands around the fat man's throat. O'Dowd lunged after Joseph and a short fracas ensued before Joseph was subdued and was frogmarched back from whence he had come, to await a more propitious moment. As he went he yelled back, 'Your card's marked, Fatso!' Which clearly offended Frank's dignity.

'I would describe myself as pleasantly plump,' he said.

Somehow, O'Dowd thought, he'd got his priorities

back to front; if it had been him he would have been more worried by the threat than the insult!

Eventually the preliminaries were completed, interview rooms assigned – one to each suspect – and the interrogations could begin. Frank and Brian each, separately, pleaded total innocence. They were honest workmen toiling for their daily crust. If anyone was to blame for the standard of the work they performed, it was the people who employed them: never prepared to pay what a more thorough job would cost, always wanting something for nothing!

'Greed,' Frank sighed. That was the trouble with the world today, everyone was too greedy.

Tommy and Rod, by contrast, each decided to duck his nut to the charge of being in possession of a stolen motor; which ought to have made things all plain sailing for Chitty and Hood who were questioning them. There was only one problem: the Cortina had quite definitely been reported stolen three days previously; but Tommy and Rod, each entirely separately, were swearing on their mother's lives that *they* had only lifted the car the day before. Which, when Chitty and Hood compared notes, only left them with one explanation. Tommy and Rod had managed to nick a car that was, in fact, already stolen!

That was only the start of their troubles.

Georgiou came to find them: a message from Sergeant Rockliffe. He requested the pleasure of their presence out in the yard – NOW!

'What for?' Hood asked.

'He says have you searched the car?' Georgiou answered.

'Gave it the once-over . . .'

'Well he says he wants it done right; with your prisoners there as witnesses. So I'd collect the bodies and get out there, toot sweet if I was you.'

There was quite a little gathering as they congregated

in the yard: Rod handcuffed to Chitty, Tommy hand-cuffed to Hood, Rockliffe there to oversee the operation and Georgiou to conduct the search. Rockliffe wanted it done right, which meant by the book and, while Georgiou might have been regarded in some quarters as a lazy bugger, too damn fond of sitting on his backside, no one could deny that he knew the book, back to front and inside out. Which is pretty well how thoroughly he searched that car: down the backs of the seats, under the seats, behind the dashboard, under the mats, inside the engine, inside the boot . . .

And it was while he was searching in the boot that he suddenly called, 'Sir . . .' Rockliffe moved round the car towards the back. The others followed. Georgiou was manhandling the spare wheel out on to the ground, and there was something not quite right about it. In fact, in the event of a puncture, it would have been useless because the tyre was half off its rim. And sticking out from inside it were what looked like bits of paper. Georgiou pushed his hand inside and, when he pulled it out, he was holding a fistful of dollar bills. The spare tyre was stuffed with them.

There was a shocked pause. Tommy was the first to break it. 'Bloody hell,' he said.

His mate, Rod, suddenly laughed harshly. 'Roll on! Talk about a fit-up!'

'Take the evidence away,' Rockliffe said quietly.

Tommy looked to him. 'You think that's worthy of you, Guv'nor? You got my record – I'm a car thief! No one's gonna believe we had anything to do with all that!'

'And them,' Rockliffe said.

Hood and Chitty gave a yank of their handcuffs.

'It's a frame!' Tommy shouted as Hood led him away. 'We're being fitted up! It's a frame!!'

Rockliffe remained for a moment, looking thoughtfully at the car; then he, too, turned and headed back into the station.

O'Dowd was getting tired of banging heads with Frank. They had started going round in circles and it was dispiriting, to say the least, to hear the same denials he had been hearing an hour before.

'Oh yeah, they want their jobs doing,' Frank was saying. 'They don't mind me risking life and limb crawling about their roofs in all weathers! But if I ended up in hospital, they wouldn't bring me grapes, would they? No! An' you try quoting 'em a fair price – they cry like babies. You can't win!'

'Fair prices,' O'Dowd said wearily. 'Come on.'

'What do you know about it?!' Frank demanded. 'You bought any slates recent? Or ally flashing? A bag of cement? Go on, tell me. Can't, can you? No. You got no idea, son!'

'You conned them, Frank,' O'Dowd said – yet again! 'You know it, we know it.' He picked up Frank's notebook from the table. 'I'm showing you your own notebook, in the name of Frank Pipe – which you admit to being your name. Half the people listed here have already lodged complaints – to us; not to the fair trading office or the building inspectorate or the Federation of Master Builders, to us! Accusing you of cheating them. And the other half will and all, given time. You've even done a chapel. A *chapel*!'

'Just 'cos it's a chapel don't mean it gets divine help,' Frank countered. 'The roof leaks!'

'I'm not surprised – after you had all the lead off it.'

'There wasn't no lead on it, an' I'm not a thief so you watch what you're saying.'

'No, you're a con merchant. You take money off people who can't afford it, an' leave 'em in a worse mess than they were to start with. And you are gonna be done for it. Fraud Squad, Frank: you keep playing that old record to me an' that's where you're going, straight over to Fraud Squad. And they're really heavy. They'll wanna see *all* your books, *all* your records. And when they've finished with 'em, you know what happens then, don't you? They pass 'em all over to the Inland Revenue, all your bank statements an' that; all your receipts, see? Inventory of all the things you own. You'll be a thin man before they've finished with you, Frank.'

Frank, for the first time, was showing slight signs of nervousness. Some of the brazen, injured innocence had gone out of his face which was, O'Dowd thought, possibly a touch paler than it had been. 'Incredible,' he thought. 'You threaten 'em with nick and they just laugh at you; you threaten 'em with the bleeding tax-man and they start to panic.'

'It's all a miscarriage of justice,' Frank was saying, 'but you can't fight it. You try and be honest, but they won't let you.' He sighed. 'Let's have a deal.'

'Deal,' O'Dowd said, suspiciously.

'I'll put something your way, you put something mine.'

'We don't work like that.'

'What are you? One-offs or something?!' Frank demanded incredulously.

'You got something to tell me, just tell me!'

There was a pause. Frank was eyeing him, trying to decide whether what he had was too valuable to risk for no guaranteed return. He must have decided it wasn't because, eventually, he said, 'Yeah, well, that foreign bloke with woodworm in his window . . . Zimmerman, was it?'

'Zimmerman – yeah? . . .'

'He's got a shooter. One of them German ones, Luger, innit? And the ammo to go with it.'

He waited, expectantly, for O'Dowd's reaction which, when it came, was a big disappointment.

'How do you know?'

'Cos I went in for a pee,' Frank said awkwardly. 'I mean, the window was out an' I got took short. So I just went in for a pee. Saw it in a drawer – ' and before O'Dowd could leap on that one he added, 'The drawer *was* open, of course.'

O'Dowd nodded. It wasn't much; it was something, it was curious, but it wasn't the stuff that deals were made of.

'I'll tell my Guv'nor,' he said, and rose to indicate that the interview was over.

He could hear Rockliffe long before he reached the squad office. Somebody was being roasted and it was vintage stuff. Somebody other than himself for once, he reflected with grim gallows humour. Whoever it was, he was glad not to be in their shoes for once, because it wasn't actually funny at all, not for him and certainly not for them. He entered the room, which strictly speaking he shouldn't have done – not with that going on; but he reckoned that Frank's bit of news might just be excuse enough to warrant the intrusion and whoever was on the receiving end might thank him for it.

It was Chitty and Hood, both of them standing sheepishly in front of Rockliffe. 'How come?!' he was saying. 'How is it Georgiou finds what *you* should have found when you gave that car a so-called search?!'

'It was just a car robbery . . .' Hood pleaded. 'We had no reason to suspect . . .'

'No reason! No bloody reason! You pair of incompetent . . . One day when you pull some drunken or hopped up nutter in a car and he points a shotgun at you you'll start thinking of reasons why you should have done this, or that, and it'll be too late! The book!

You go by the book! You do things by the book! The *book* is bloody God! Am I getting through to you?!'

Chitty nodded. 'Sorry, Skip.'

'Me too, Guv,' Hood added.

'It won't happen again,' Chitty promised.

Rockliffe looked round sharply and saw O'Dowd standing just inside the door. 'What's the matter, O'Dowd?! You want some?!'

'No, Skip . . .'S'just, I've got something, like. That's all.'

Rockliffe looked back to the other pair. He was beginning to calm down and he rubbed the back of his neck to help ease away the tension. 'Alright,' he said. 'The stuff's probably forged in which case it'll end up with the funny money squad; or, since it's American, the FBI. But for the moment, it's ours. And I've been thinking about those two laddoes downstairs and I think they're telling the truth. I don't believe they'd've been trying to sell the car for a few hundred nicker if they'd known there was all that lot in the boot. So what we want to know is, who had the car before them? Right?'

Hood and Chitty both nodded.

'And I want some results from you pair,' Rockliffe told them, 'or I'll drop you like a ton of bricks!' He turned to O'Dowd. 'Right. What've you got that's burning a hole in your pocket?'

Briefly, O'Dowd told him. Rockliffe was hardly any more impressed than he himself had been.

'Probably a war souvenir.'

O'Dowd nodded. 'Age is about right.'

'So what are you going to do?'

'Well,' O'Dowd said, 'I don't see as there's much point hanging on to Laurel and Hardy. Lot of paper-work to make this fraud thing stick so I reckon we might as well bail 'em. Then someone ought to get round and see this Zimmerman bloke about his shooter.'

'Someone?' Rockliffe queried. 'Why not you?'

'I've a meet this afters, Skip.'

Rockliffe nodded. 'Adams, then. You'd better brief him.'

'What about a warrant?' O'Dowd asked. 'The old boy wasn't too helpful this morning.'

'I do believe you're starting to use your noddle, O'Dowd,' Rockliffe said approvingly. 'Tell Adams to get a W sorted. And he can take Walsh. She doesn't seem to be doing much.'

O'Dowd nodded.

'Right,' Rockliffe said. 'So we all know what we're doing?' There were general nods of assent. 'Then what are we standing here for?!'

There was a general rush for the door.

9

'What's all this then?' Tommy exclaimed, as Chitty snapped on the cuffs.

Standing in the cell doorway, Hood said, 'You're gonna show us where you chored the motor.'

'What? . . .' Tommy said. 'I told you where!'

'No, you're not listening, son,' Hood explained patiently. 'I said "show us". And I mean – *show* us, *exactly*, where. Got it?'

'You mean you're taking me to Balham?' Tommy asked, and the idea didn't seem to fill him with much enthusiasm.

'That's right,' Chitty said. 'Nice little outing.' He led Tommy towards the door.

'You don't know what you're doing to me,' Tommy groaned, which made no sense to either Hood or Chitty, not that either of them particularly cared.

In the car, Tommy grew quieter the nearer they came to Balham and, entering the street in which he claimed the car had been parked, Chitty was aware that Tommy had slid down in his seat so that he was as low as he could get without actually being on the floor.

'What you doing down there?' Chitty asked.

'My manor, ain't it?' Tommy replied grudgingly. 'I don't wanna be seen with you lot, do I?'

'This the street?' Hood queried.

'Yeah.'

'So where was it parked when you nicked it?'

'About halfway down, on the right.'

Hood looked. It was a residential street of old, Victorian semis, some in quite reasonable nick, others badly in need of a lick of paint. There were small front

70

gardens, several of which had been turned into hard-standing for cars. The trees along the kerb were still in leaf, affording dappled shade. It had about it a quiet, almost sleepy air.

'Half-way down on the right,' Hood repeated. 'Yeah, but where *exactly*?'

'I don't know, do I?' Tommy pleaded. 'Look, do we have to hang about? I've shown you where we chored the motor, so can't we just . . .'

'What's the matter with you?!' Hood interjected. 'You look sick! Are you sick? What's the matter, eh?!'

'I'm scared, ain't I?' Tommy said.

'What of?!' Chitty asked in some surprise.

'Them geezers! You find 'em, they'll eat you!'

'What geezers?!' Hood demanded, starting to become very impatient.

'The geezers that were in the car!'

Hood and Chitty exchanged a glance. What was he saying? What hadn't he told them?

'You never mentioned any geezers in the bloody car!' Hood accused him.

'You never asked! Anyway, it's self-preservation, mate; they was a dead nasty-looking team. If I hadn't been half shant I'd've left 'em alone. Can we go now?'

The answer was – no! Not till this had been well sorted, because if Tommy had actually seen the men from whom he had stolen the car, he had probably also seen the men responsible for the dollar bills.

'You're telling us,' Hood said slowly, 'that there was some geezers in that car when . . .'

'When I spotted it, parked,' Tommy took over, desperate to get the tale told so that they could start off again and depart. 'Two of 'em, in the back. The other one, big as an 'ouse, came later, out of the travel agency.'

Another revelation!

'What travel agency?' Hood almost shouted.

'The one it was parked outside of!'

'Can we get this clear?' Chitty asked. 'You saw it parked outside a travel agency. Then it drove to this street, and after the occupants had got out, you nicked it?'

'Well, I wouldn't nick it with them in it, would I?' Tommy said, reasonably.

'So where'd they go when they got out?' Hood asked. 'Into a house? Where?'

Tommy nodded.

'Which one?'

'Look,' Tommy pleaded. 'I feel vulnerable, right? Like I told you, I was shant. The model fitted my bent paperwork, otherwise I wouldn't've touched it. Now you drive me back to the nick, bang me up, and then I'll tell you the house.'

'What d'you think we are?!' Hood roared, 'a bleedin' taxi service?! Now if you don't tell us which drum, I'm gonna walk you up and down this street with the cuffs on! Till we find it!'

Tommy caved in. 'I don't know the number, only it had a wooden milk thing outside – four holes for milk bottles and a number you could turn on top – how many pints you wanted. I noticed it. I wanted it for me mum, only it was chained up. They went in there.'

'Mind him,' Hood told Chitty, and opened his door.

'You gonna nick 'em?' Tommy asked in disbelief.

'I wouldn't be surprised,' Hood said.

'I would. You haven't seen 'em, mate.'

Hood slammed his door and crossed the street. Being the middle of the afternoon, it was quiet and still. In fact, Hood was aware that other than a cat on one of the garden walls, he was the only living thing in the street and it made him feel conspicuous, slightly uneasy. If there was anyone looking from behind any of those net curtains, anyone with half an ounce of criminal perception, they would make him for what he was in no time flat. It made him doubt the wisdom of what he was doing, but he didn't fancy giving Tommy the satisfaction of seeing him chicken so, trying to look as though a copper was the last thing in the world he could possibly be, he kept on going.

Outside the front door of one of the houses, about half-way down the road, true to Tommy's word, there was a wooden milk container chained to the step. Hood paused, briefly, to take in the house. It looked ordinary enough; could do with some redecorating; the garden was a bit scraggy but by no means completely neglected. It wasn't until Hood's eyes were sweeping over the frontage for a second time that he suddenly caught sight of the small notice in the downstairs window. It read: 'Vacancies'. 'A boarding house,' he thought. 'Nice one.' And with rather more confidence now in his step, he approached the front door.

It was answered by a woman in her fifties, widow, he guessed, supplementing her dear, deceased's pension, and probably not bothering to tell the tax-man, either. She certainly viewed his warrant card with what could have been taken for distinct misgivings. But when she learnt that his interest was in her lodgers, her manner changed remarkably. Fancy him calling, she said; she had been meaning to get on to the police herself only what with one thing and then another; fancy him being interested in *them*, she said, not that it surprised her, not in the least. No, they weren't still with her – that was the point, they'd left the day before, and without settling up, first . . .

As Hood climbed back into the car, Chitty said, 'Well?'

'Done a bunk. Soon as Bright Eyes there nicked the car, it seems.'

'That's a relief.' Tommy breathed a mite more easily.

Hood turned to him. 'So: this travel agency you saw

'em come out of; you take us.' And he started up the car.

Old Mr Zimmerman admitted Adams and Karen Walsh without any fuss. Indeed, there was something almost extraordinary about the effect the sight of the search warrant had on him. He simply meekly obeyed, without question or demur, as though that piece of paper removed from him any vestige of self-assertion or right, even, to protest.

The room in which they found themselves, well . . . it was dark to start with, thanks to the window still being boarded up. The furniture was mostly old and heavy, but it was clean and the surfaces shone, and there was no mustiness or staleness, which spoke well for the old man's fastidiousness in his housework. Adams and Karen were so busy taking it in that they failed to notice Zimmerman extracting a wooden box from the sideboard drawer. It wasn't until he spoke that their attention returned to him, and they saw with a jolt that he was holding the gun and that it was pointing in their direction.

'Is this what you are looking for?' he asked.

Adams and Karen exchanged a flick of a glance. Docile, old gentlemen holding Lugers could prove to be just as unstable, just as screwy, just as dangerous as a doped up addict with a knife at your throat.

'Yes, that seems to be it, sir,' Adams said evenly, trying to keep his voice very calm. 'Would you . . . would you like to put it down, please?'

Zimmerman looked to the gun and it seemed, almost, to take him by surprise that he was pointing it. He laid it on the table, along with its box and moved back to allow Adams to reach it.

'Is it loaded, Mr Zimmerman?' Karen asked.

'Of course,' he replied, as though to have a gun

which was not loaded would be to be guilty of a contradiction in terms.

'Is the, er . . . is the safety on?' Adams enquired, still reluctant to pick the Luger up.

'I'm not sure,' the old man replied and made a move as though to pick the gun up again, but Adams slid it across the table away from him. 'I was just going to show you, you may release the magazine from the butt, if you wish,' Zimmerman explained patiently.

'Yes, thank you,' Karen said and, to Adams' surprise, she picked it up herself. 'Here?' Zimmerman nodded. Karen pressed the button and the magazine slid out into her hand. As she laid it down again she caught Adams' face. 'Well, I was never much for playing with dolls, you know,' she said by way of explanation. 'All boys in my family, gun-mad. So something was bound to rub off.'

Adams smiled and looked back to the old man. 'It's German, isn't it? And you're German, I take it, Mr Zimmerman. It means . . . carpenter, doesn't it? Your name? In German?'

Zimmerman didn't respond. He just sat at the table and put his head in his hands.

'Would you like to tell us about the gun, sir?' Adams persisted.

'Expect it's a war memento,' Karen suggested. 'My uncle had one. Only he filed the firing pin off his.'

'That right, is it, sir?' Adams said. 'That what it is? A war memento?'

'Memento,' Zimmerman said, almost to himself. 'I need a memento – tah!'

'Then what? You tell us. We're just asking.' The old man didn't respond. Adams and Karen exchanged another glance. He wasn't being what you might call helpful, not exactly forthcoming. And there was something about him, his utter passivity and defeated air, that neither of them could understand. Adams picked up the box which had housed the gun and looked inside. It contained nothing but a piece of very old, well-fingermarked, tatty paper. Adams took it out. The writing on it was in ink which was faded now, so that he had difficulty in making out the words. The difficulty was compounded, he realized, by the fact that it was in German. He had taken German at school and had passed his 'O' level in it; but that seemed a long time ago now, and he hadn't had any occasion to make use of it since then, so that he was more than just a little rusty.

'To a . . . Gunter?' he read. 'Gunter Gold . . .'

'Gunter Goldschmidt,' Zimmerman said flatly. He held out his hand for the piece of paper. 'Shall I read it for you?'

'Please.' Adams handed it over.

Zimmerman didn't even look at it. He just held it limply on his knee while he stared away, into the past. 'The note ends,' he said eventually, 'with a prayer for the soul of Gunter Goldschmidt. It starts . . . with a judgement for Gunter Goldschmidt, and the judgement is death.'

For several moments afterwards you could have heard a pin drop in the room and the air seemed suddenly to have turned very cold. Zimmerman hadn't moved. That he knew the note off by heart was self-evident; that it wearied and oppressed and sickened him to his very soul was equally evident from his voice.

'Who is Gunter Goldschmidt?' Karen asked softly. He didn't answer. 'Are you Gunter Goldschmidt?' He didn't answer.

'I think you had better come with us, sir,' Adams said finally.

Wearily but dutifully, Zimmerman rose from his chair. His eyes cast around for his jacket and Karen handed it to him from the chair, and helped him as he shrugged it on. He suddenly seemed to have shrunk,

76

even since they had been with him, so that it hung on him and he looked drowned in it.

'They were young men, much like yourself,' he told Adams quietly. 'Their uniforms immaculate; they were frightening in their perfection, their arrogance.'

'Who were?' Adams said. Once again the old man declined to answer. 'You don't have to tell us about it,' Adams said, 'but I have to tell you that I'm arresting you for being in unlawful possession of a firearm.'

Tommy sat in the Collator office and stared wretchedly at the photographs they had placed before him. He couldn't work out how it had come to this. All he had done was steal a car, just a normal, everyday bit of business. And yet now here he was, not only nicked but being forced into doing something that was probably very unhealthy, personally speaking, and went against all his principles! It didn't seem right. If only he'd never seen that bloody motor!

'I told you, I was shant!' he pleaded.

Hood, standing behind him, lent forward over his shoulder. 'Not so drunk you couldn't drive a vehicle off, and you've already described the bloke to the travel agent. Take your time, Tommy; we've got bags of that here.'

Tommy regarded the photographs for another, unhappy moment. 'It sickens me,' he said.

'What does?'

'I mean, what does this make me? A bloody grass!'

'Your choice, cocker,' Hood returned, with scant sympathy.

'Choice?! You call that a choice?! Cop for something I don't know nothing about, or finger some other geezer!? That's being forced, mate, coerced, unfair pressure!'

'Forced? . . .' Hood gave a laugh. 'Listen pal – and

77

this is off the record – you don't need to *force* anyone to grass, not these days. You're out of date if you think that. Nowadays you get killed in the bleeding stampede! It's all a matter of who grasses first, innit?'

Tommy thought about that for a moment then gave a sigh. 'Yeah, I suppose you're right,' he said sadly. He pointed to one of the photographs. 'That's the geezer.'

10

'Baker,' Rockliffe said, regarding the photograph and CR file. 'George Edward Baker.' The face that stared back at him from the photograph was of a big, ugly man, the kind that most folk would prefer not to meet on a dark night. 'He's never been mixed up with funny money before – not that we know of. Sure it's him?'

Hood assured him that it was. Both the landlady and the travel agent had confirmed the description; but just for good measure the photograph was now on its way over to be shown to them both for a positive ID. Karen Walsh had come across from her desk to have a look.

'My God, he's a gorilla,' she said.

'Nearest thing to it you'll find outside a zoo,' Rockliffe agreed.

According to the travel agent, Hood informed him, Baker had bought a cross-channel ticket for himself and his car for the day before. So it looked as though he had a buyer for the dollars somewhere in France.

'Only we've got the dollars,' Rockliffe said. 'So did he go?'

'Not according to the passenger list,' Hood told him.

'Right,' Rockliffe said. 'Means he's still here.' He handed Baker's file back to Hood. 'You want to check if he's back at the address on this file. It's his mum's house, so get a W 'cos she won't let you in.'

'Right, Guv.'

'And when you've got the W sorted, let me know, 'cos I fancy coming along myself on this one. We'll take you, me, Chitty, Georgiou . . .'

'I'm free,' Karen said hopefully.

Rockliffe and Hood glanced at each other. 'Why not?' Rockliffe said. Hood nodded and headed for the door. Rockliffe turned to Karen. 'Alright, then: so where's this Zimmerman or whatever he calls himself?'

'Interview room, Skip. Dave's with him.'

Rockliffe nodded and moved towards the door. 'You, too,' he said. 'You were one of the arresting officers.'

Karen followed, and as they went she gave Rockliffe, again, a resumé of their odd and disquieting interview with the old man.

Zimmerman was sitting, his head bowed, as Rockliffe and Karen entered. An untouched cup of coffee was on the table in front of him. Adams was sitting to one side with a blank statement form in front of him. He looked both bored and mystified. He gave Rockliffe a small shake of his head indicating that there had been no communication. Rockliffe drew up a chair and sat opposite Zimmerman who, still, hadn't raised his head. Karen sat down beside Adams.

Rockliffe regarded the old man for a moment then said, in a gentle voice, 'Your coffee's getting cold, Mr Zimmerman.' The old man didn't move or respond in any way. Rockliffe waited for a moment before, in the same gently cajoling voice, saying, 'This isn't getting us anywhere, is it, sir – now is it?'

Zimmerman slowly raised his head. 'You are in charge?'

Rockliffe nodded with an encouraging, friendly smile. 'Detective Sergeant Rockliffe.'

'They are so young, your er . . .' Zimmerman's gaze travelled across to Karen and Adams.

Rockliffe permitted himself a little chuckle. 'There's the old saying, isn't there? When the policemen start looking young you know you must be getting older. Now then, Mr Zimmerman, the custody officer tells me you won't co-operate with the custody record; you won't speak to my officers. It's not helping to get this thing sorted out, you know? And that's what we all want, to get it sorted out and to get about our business.'

It couldn't have been more reasonable, or done in a more reasonable way. But Zimmerman had bowed his head again and it was back to where they had started.

Adopting a sterner tone, Rockliffe said, 'Sir, I want you to explain to me why you were in possession of an unlicensed fire-arm, which is a custodial offence in this country. A very serious offence.' Rockliffe paused; nothing was forthcoming. 'Is your name, in fact, Zimmerman?' Nothing. 'How long have you been resident in this country?' No response.

Adams and Karen were exchanging a glance. They had never come across anything quite like this before and, frustrating and infuriating as it was, it was mystifying and intriguing as well. There was something about the old man, an aura that he gave off, which endowed him with a sense of tragedy. It was possible, Karen found, actually to sympathize with him without knowing why or for what; simply because of the blackness that was inside him and weighing on him and which made, presumably, in his eyes, communication an irrelevancy.

'Look, sir,' Rockliffe said, 'I can go through the aliens registry at Lunar House, only you must understand that that takes time. You must also understand that I am in a position to hold you in custody for unlawful possession of a firearm. You could be remanded in prison, until we find out your true identity. But I don't think either of us wants it to come to that, do we?'

Zimmerman spoke! Only it took them a moment to realize that that was what was happening because his voice was very low and his head remained bowed.

'My name is Gunter Goldschmidt. I was born in Germany in 1921. I am Jewish.'

81

'I see,' Rockliffe said, with a hint of relief in his voice.

Zimmerman – or Goldschmidt since that was his real name – slowly looked up and smiled a weary smile. 'Do you? No, I don't think you do. To be Jewish in Adolf Hitler's Germany was a crime.'

'Yes,' Rockliffe said. 'Terrible.' While, in his own mind, he was already concluding that Gunter Goldschmidt was just another of those unfortunate old folk, whose grasp on life was becoming tenuous and for whom the past had superseded the present.

'Six million,' Goldschmidt was saying with an incredulous tone to his voice. 'Six million murdered; the world went mad.'

'You were a prisoner of the Nazis, I take it?' Rockliffe said, trying to help him along.

But Goldschmidt, now he had once started, wasn't going to be hurried or have his tale told for him – not that anyone could have done so. It was rooted in the past, but it stretched to the present, and to understand the present one also had to understand the past. That was his responsibility: if the tale was to be told at all, it had to be understood, all of it.

'There were some of us,' he said, 'who avoided capture until quite late in the war. Not all Germans shared the madman's opinion of what was called the Jewish "problem". Some of us were hidden, cared for by the ordinary Germans – and by our own race. These good people took considerable risks. They did it in the name of humanity, knowing the danger. They were good, brave people.'

'A very terrible episode in history, Herr Goldschmidt,' Rockliffe concurred, placing slight emphasis on the word 'history'.

Goldschmidt noticed and smiled. 'History to you.'

'Look, sir,' Rockliffe said, 'although I sympathize –

and I truly do – all we are interested in, here and now is . . .'

'Gunter Goldschmidt,' the old man suggested.

'Yes. And the gun.'

'The gun was because Gunter Goldschmidt was a coward.' Rockliffe was displaying slight signs of restiveness, but Goldschmidt continued in his own way, at his own pace. 'To live as a coward can be worse than to die as a man.'

'Lordy, Lordy,' Adams thought, 'now it's riddles as well!' and he looked at Rockliffe to see how he was taking it.

Goldschmidt was still speaking, telling of the horror of the death camps, but this time Rockliffe was determined to get to the nub of the affair. 'Mr Goldschmidt . . . Mr Goldschmidt!' Goldschmidt paused. 'Why,' Rockliffe asked, 'do you want a gun?'

So Goldschmidt told him. And his voice was so tired and so old and yet so remorseless, it made it all the more dreadful. After his capture, in order to preserve his own life, he had informed on others: families which were hidden, and the people who were hiding them. Personally he had been responsible, in this way, for a great many murders. And in this way, he had survived through to the liberation. But then he had been denounced, tried and condemned by his own people; and that sentence was what was written on the paper in the box. He had been given the gun and the instruction. But then he had fled to this country and here he had remained.

'The gun was to kill yourself with? Is that what you're saying?' Rockliffe asked flatly.

Goldschmidt nodded. 'But I did not. I was a coward once; I will not be a coward again. I will live; and I will remember.'

There was quite a pause after that. Noises intruded, from the corridor and from the yard outside but somehow, within the room itself, it was as if everything had stopped; just for a moment, as though time and the whole rhythm of the universe had come to a standstill.

Rockliffe coughed awkwardly. 'I see. Well . . . Herr Goldschmidt, obviously the gun will be held by us and destroyed. In view of what you have just told us, I am recommending that you be bailed pending enquiries. Adams, take Mr Goldschmidt back to the CO.'

Adams stretched his legs and lifted himself to his feet.

Karen Walsh suddenly found it necessary to use her handkerchief.

They approached the house in two cars, Rockliffe in one, Hood, Chitty, Georgiou and Karen in the other. They parked with about ten yards between them, both on the opposite side of the road and both out of direct eye-line of the downstairs windows.

It was starting to get dark. Most people were indoors and there were lights on in the other council houses round about though, in most cases, the curtains weren't yet drawn so that as their eyes scanned the street it was as though they were seeing a disconnected sequence of screen showing disjointed, disconnected fragments of disconnected lives. It was at odd moments like this that Rockliffe, in the disjointed isolation of his own fucked-up life, gained a perception of the ordinary human condition that would have sent a man with willpower any less than his straight back to the bottle again.

He pulled himself together and concentrated on Baker's house: lights on in the side back, and in the hall. No car outside. No sign that Baker was in there, one way or the other.

Rockliffe climbed out of his car, locked his door, and walked back to where the others were parked.

Clouds were blowing up and there was the promise of rain. He hunched, his hands in his jacket pockets. Autumn was the season he felt his loneliness most of all.

He crouched by the open driver's window. 'Well?'

Within, everyone's eyes settled on Hood.

'What you all looking at me for?!' he demanded, not relishing the thought of being the first to confront Baker.

'Your warrant,' Rockliffe said. 'You sussed him out.' He turned to Georgiou. 'You, round the back.'

'Right,' Georgiou said. He climbed out of the car. 'I'm going for a walk now. And I might be some time.'

'If he comes out your way, all you have to do is stop him,' Rockliffe said. 'Then yell for us.'

Georgiou cast his eyes to the heavens and set off across the road. Reluctantly, Hood climbed out after him.

'Likely isn't even in there,' he said.

'Won't be, we go in team-handed,' Rockliffe assured him.

They gave Georgiou time to get round to the back, then Hood started walking towards the house. Rockliffe gave a nod to the others, and they unlatched their doors in readiness. They saw Hood go through the gate and up to the front door where he knocked. His wait wasn't a long one. The door opened and against the hallway light they saw the figure of a giant of a man. It wasn't necessary to be able to distinguish his features clearly in order to know that it was Baker. They saw Hood apparently hesitate, then produce his warrant card and hold it up. They saw Baker take a step out of the house towards him.

'Here we go!' Rockliffe said, and started running.

Chitty burst out of the car, followed, with not quite so much alacrity, by Karen. Rockliffe had the start on them, but it was Chitty who reached the gate first.

Baker, suddenly becoming aware of the running figures, had turned and lunged desperately back inside the house. He swung the front door to slam it on them, but Hood had the presence of mind to get his boot in the jamb and Baker was still bashing the door against it as Chitty charged.

Live to be a hundred, they would still talk about that moment. It earned an instant place in squad folklore, to be passed on to future generations with pride and awe; the moment that was remembered simply as Chitty's Charge.

What was his inspiration? Even he wasn't sure; except he remembered that once he had seen an enraged bull smash clean through a five-bar gate. Whether that was his example or not, his performance was remarkably similar. He came down the garden path at full tilt and, without breaking stride, hit the door. The impact took it clean off its hinges. Baker, behind it, was slammed back by a seemingly unimaginable force. He fell, concussed; the door crashed on top of him; and Chitty came last, careering right over him, to end up in an untidy, somewhat surprised heap at the far end of the hall.

Surveying the debris of the door and Baker as Rockliffe and Karen arrived, Hood said, 'I was just about to do that.' Then he stepped inside to start sorting out the pieces.

Much later that evening, as they were leaving the station, Georgiou, Karen and Janice Hargreaves experienced another, more minor, collision of bodies. This time, it was fat Frank, the fraudulent master builder, who was dashing in as they were going out, closely followed by his leaner compatriot, Brian. Both were panting and both looked genuinely frightened.

'Here,' Frank gasped as he recovered his breath.

'We don't want bail no more! There's a bunch of bloody Zulus out there with whacking great big knives!'

'Zulus?! . . .' Georgiou exclaimed.

'That Maxwell kid and his mates! Talk about Rorke's Drift, I think we need protection!'

Janice sighed. 'Don't even bother getting one in for me,' she advised Georgiou and Karen, then she turned to the two builders. 'Do I take it you are formally accusing someone of threatening you with physical violence?'

'Too bloody right we are!' Frank told her.

She nodded. She had been afraid of that.

11

'What d'you reckon?' Rockliffe said.

He was holding a delicate, intricate gold bracelet which he had taken from a jiffy bag on his lap. He seemed . . . awkward about it, a little embarrassed, perhaps. Janice took the bracelet and examined it. The workmanship was beautiful.

''S great, Skip,' she said. She wouldn't have minded if someone had bought that for her. 'What's this here? K.R.? That her initials?'

Rockliffe nodded. 'Kate. Kate Rockliffe. Kathleen, really.'

'Seen what it looks like on?'

'Only on the assistant.'

'Can I?' Janice wanted to try it on.

Rockliffe nodded and looked back to the scene beyond the car's window. They were parked in a street close to the corner where it entered a small, somewhat run-down square. Most of the houses had been converted to flats; one or two were still having their innards ripped out of them with skips of rubble standing in the road and scaffolding obscuring their fronts. There were also two or three down-market hotels and it was one of these that Rockliffe and his team were watching.

Parked at the kerb outside was a tourist bus proclaiming, 'Melkveg Tours, Utrecht' from stickers in its windows. The German holidaymakers it was about to take on board were emerging from the hotel in dribs and drabs and congregating on the pavement, while a small mountain of suitcases and bags built up at the rear of the bus. It had started to rain. They looked a tired, dejected bunch, huddling under brollies and inside anoraks.

'Good-bye to London,' Rockliffe said sarcastically. 'A holiday to remember. They've been conned, ripped-off and poisoned. It's pissed on their heads for ten days. And now, just when they thought the nightmare was over, some joker's coming to blag their suitcase.'

Or that, at least, is what the word was. There had been a particularly concentrated spate of thefts from tourists over the last few weeks and the whisper that had reached Rockliffe was that this was to be the scene of the next. He had a name, too: Sinclair. But what he wanted, what he needed, was to catch him at it.

He glanced back to Janice. Against her brown arm the bracelet looked stunning.

'Reckon she'll like it?' he asked.

'Yeah!' She took it off and handed it back.

'Bloody better,' Rockliffe said.

'How much they rush you for that, then?'

'Too much. Still, you're only eighteen once. Got tickets for the theatre and all. Saturday. Best stall seats.' He returned the bracelet, inside its jiffy bag, into his pocket, then he looked back to the square and yawned. 'Well come on, then, if you're coming!'

Rockliffe wasn't the only one to become impatient. In a first-floor room of one of the other hotels in the square, whose windows afforded a clear view of the tourist bus, Georgiou and Karen Walsh were also watching and waiting. Or, rather, Karen was watching and Georgiou was waiting. She was at the window with binoculars while he lounged on one of the beds. Both were dressed rather more smartly than the place or the occasion might have seemed to demand. But their cover was that of a honeymoon couple and both had done their best to look the part. Unfortunately, as they now realized, in a dump like this it only made them stand out all the more. Also unfortunate, at least as far as Georgiou was concerned, was that Karen didn't seem particularly interested in living out their cover to any further degree. Disgruntled, he bounced on the bed and sourly surveyed the room.

'Thirty-five quid,' he grumbled – as though the money had actually come out of his own pocket. 'Honeymoon couple? Whoever's idea that was must have a funny sense of humour. Only couple likely to come here'd be paying for a quick one, or a couple of nutters, on the run from Rampton.'

'Speak for yourself, Georgiou,' Karen told him.

'I mean, look at this bed. It's got lumps! One leg's shorter than the other! Look!' Karen was too busy watching the square. 'People top themselves in rooms like this, you know?'

'Paul,' Karen said suddenly. 'I think we've got a live one.'

In their car, Rockliffe and Janice had seen the same thing: a battered Sunbeam Alpine had turned into the far side of the square and had stopped. Its driver was a West Indian. In the passenger seat, difficult to distinguish from this angle, was a white girl and there was someone in the back, too.

'That Billy?' Janice asked, meaning the driver.

'Eric,' Rockliffe answered. 'Brother Eric.' He picked up his PR. 'Better wake up, One-Two. Sorry to disturb your nuptials, only we've got company. Yellow Alpine. Clocked 'em?'

'Roger, One-One.' Karen came back.

'The driver's Eric Sinclair. Slippery as a bucket of eels, so watch it,' Rockliffe told his PR. 'Should be a white bloke and a girl who do the actual business. They'll be carrying dummy suitcases and the second they dump 'em by the bus, you make your way down to the street. We'll drive round and block their exit, by which time you'll be in position so we can lift them; all four of us, won't you, One-One? Georgiou listening?'

'He's listening,' Karen assured him.

They watched the Alpine softly nose around the square, looking for a parking spot closer to the bus. When it finally stopped it was only a matter of twenty or so yards from where Rockliffe and Janice were sitting. Sure enough, out from the back climbed a young white bloke who joined his girlfriend on the pavement as Eric, the driver, unloaded a couple of suitcases from the boot.

'There we go,' Rockliffe said softly. 'Best Taiwan cardboard.'

Eric climbed back into the car, while the couple set off up the street, lugging the suitcases with them.

'Look heavy,' Janice observed.

'Yeah,' Rockliffe agreed. 'Housebricks are.'

From her vantage point at the hotel window, Karen watched the couple's progress towards the bus. 'Any minute now,' she told Georgiou. Just then, from one of the adjoining rooms, there was the sound of a crash as though a table had been knocked over and, a moment later, the radio in the room was turned up loud. Georgiou and Karen exchanged a questioning glance. 'More honeymooners?' Karen suggested ironically.

'Having more fun than we are, anyway,' Georgiou replied.

Certainly something was going on next door; because, even despite the volume of radio, they could hear loud voices and more thumps of furniture. 'Showing her who's boss, right from the start,' Georgiou concluded, but Karen wasn't sure it was that funny. If this other business wasn't so near to coming off . . . She returned her gaze to the street.

It was at about the same moment that Rockliffe clocked the fact that Eric Sinclair, in the Alpine, was looking in their direction somewhat intently.

'Come on Hargreaves,' Rockliffe muttered, 'time for a cuddle.'

Which, momentarily, took her somewhat by surprise, but then she realized what he meant, and they embraced one another in an attempt not to look conspicuous. With her face buried in Rockliffe's shoulder Janice wished she'd come armed with a gas mask because his jacket positively reeked, of smoke and tobacco and beer and God knows what else!

'Take a shufty,' he said.

Slowly she raised her face. Eric was still looking directly at them. Their eyes met; and, for no earthly reason she could ever explain, Janice simply became transfixed, entirely incapable of looking away. In Eric's mind, it confirmed the worst. He suddenly banged his horn twice in warning and started the Alpine. The couple with the suitcases hesitated for a split second, then simply dropped the cases and started running back towards the car.

'I've blown it,' said Janice, stricken.

From her window, Karen could see that something had gone wrong. But that was suddenly less important than what was going on next door. Even over the radio they could hear a man's voice shouting, beseeching, crying and then screaming in the instant before there were two unmistakable gun shots. The scream stopped abruptly. Karen and Georgiou's eyes met for the briefest moment and then they were diving for the door.

As Karen flung it open, two men careered past, making for the stairs. She yelled at them. The first didn't pause, was already at the staircase but the man behind him, bulkier and slower, swung viciously towards Karen and Georgiou, raising his right arm as he did so. It held the gun. There is something about having a gun pointed at you – a real one – particularl in the hands of someone you know has already jus fired it; even a seasoned copper will tell you that. There are also ways of dealing with it: Georgiou's and Karen's was prudent, if not entirely text-book; they simply ducked back inside their room again, flattening themselves beside the door. By the time Karen risked another glance out the man had gone. Georgiou was already gabbling into his PR, as Karen, bravely, went in pursuit of them.

'Skip, there's a little bloke and a big bloke leaving the hotel! We've just heard two shots, and the big one's got a firearm! . . .'

Rockliffe didn't know what was coming down. Janice was already accelerating the Astra forward, but too late to stop the Alpine containing the three luggage thieves. It squealed across their bows, spun broadside to them, and was off up the street in which they had been parked. At the same time Rockliffe could see two figures, men, one slight the other much bulkier, tearing out of the hotel in which Karen and Georgiou were positioned, and heading for a Volvo parked at the kerb.

'Round! Keep going!' Rockliffe said.

The men were scrambling into the car. Karen had emerged from the hotel behind them and, from the top of the steps, was shouting, 'Stop them! Stop those men! . . .' The smaller man was gunning the Volvo to start as the Astra passed it and Janice slammed on the anchors, swerving the car diagonally across the street to block the getaway.

The Volvo had started. Rockliffe leaped out of the Astra and lunged round towards it. But the Volvo didn't stop. It ploughed straight into the side of the police car and simply kept on going, shunting it broadside down the street. Rockliffe snatched at the Volvo's door handle but it tore out of his grasp.

'Janice! . . .' Karen yelled, wide-eyed with fear, as she saw her friend being bulldozed away in the Astra.

Rockliffe had produced his stick from his inside pocket and he hurled it at the back window of the Volvo. It merely bounced off. One of the German tourists had come running into the road and was crouching with his camera, snapping off shots of the excitement for all he was worth.

At last, at last! the Astra slanted away from the Volvo allowing it to scrape past with an awful grating, teeth-piercing noise of metal against metal. And then the Volvo was accelerating away to the end of the square where it swerved around the corner and out of sight.

Rockliffe and Karen raced towards the stationary Astra. Within, Janice could be seen sitting, white-faced and blank with shock but apparently otherwise unhurt. Rockliffe dragged open her door.

'The number?! Did you get the number?! . . .'

'Sorry? . . .' Hargreaves sounded vague, far away.

'The registration number – MK something. Did you see it?!'

Janice tried to focus on what Rockliffe was saying, but she felt dizzy and sick and numb.

'Come on, Skip,' Karen complained on Janice's behalf.

'What? . . .' he said. 'Oh, yeah. You okay, Hargreaves?'

'Yeah . . . Never felt better, as it happens,' she replied, slowly coming back to them, as it were. She raised her left hand and she had a gash across the back of it which was bleeding freely.

'Yeah, well,' Rockliffe said, a bit awkwardly, and he reached across her for the car's radio. 'Victor Charlie One-One to MP – urgent call . . .' He stopped, suddenly realizing that there had been neither static nor carrier wave; the radio was dead, another victim of the shunt. He looked at the two girls. 'Come on,' he said irritably, and headed back towards the hotel, taking

94

out his PR as he went. 'Victor Charlie One-One to Control, this is a call for urgent assistance . . .'

Whilst all of this had been happening, Georgiou, bracing himself, had ventured into the next-door room. The sight which had greeted him had turned his stomach over. The wardrobe was half overturned, wedged against a wall. There were fresh, copious blood stains on the bed, particularly around the pillow; and there was a man, middle-aged in a suit and tie, on his hands and crawling slowly, weakly across the floor towards him. The man had a gunshot wound in his neck from which blood was pumping in rhythmical spurts. The carpet was soaked with it.

Georgiou was no expert on injuries or woundings, but he knew a bad one when he saw it and he had never seen anything as bad as that. The rate at which the man was losing blood, he couldn't have much more left in him. Getting the better of his stomach, Georgiou desperately ripped one of the sheets off the bed then went down on his knees beside the man, taking his head into his lap as he tried to staunch the wound. It was unquenchable.

'Who did it, eh?' he asked with gentle urgency. 'Who were they? Can you tell me, old chap? Were they friends of yours?'

The man tried to speak but his strength was ebbing, and all that came out was a kind of gasp. Desperately Georgiou pressed the sodden sheet to the wound even harder. And that's how he still was when Rockliffe arrived.

'He's going, Skip,' Georgiou told him. He drew away the sheet for Rockliffe to see. 'It's there, see.' Rockliffe nodded. 'I've done all I can.' It wasn't self-justification; it was just a sad, resigned statement of his own inadequacy.

'Sure,' Rockliffe said. He crouched beside the man whose eyes were open, frightened, staring at him.

Rockliffe gently waved his hand in front of the man's face and the eyes blinked. 'Listen,' Rockliffe said, 'we want a name, just one name, okay? The boy who shot you, who was he?'

The man managed a very slight nod, but then his eyes closed and he passed beyond their helping.

'Bugger it,' Rockliffe said softly.

12

The murder of Peter Thorne – the name found on the credit cards in his wallet – took precedence over everything. That was how the Crime Squad operated. For most of the time they were free to pursue their own ends and whatever Rockliffe deemed was suitable and best for them. But as soon as a major incident occurred they were simply absorbed into the general pool of manpower required for the operation.

Thorne's murder could have proved to be a long and difficult case. He was forty-one years old, married, company director of a small paper-and-packaging firm in Staines. He had no police record; he was not, so far as could be ascertained, on anyone's list of known associates and had never, as far as anyone knew, put a foot out of line in his life. So what he was doing in the bedroom of a seedy Paddington hotel, copping a ·38 bullet in the neck, was a total mystery. He had, what was more, no known enemies, either business or personal, so the motive for his killing was equally a mystery. The only odd thing about him that preliminary investigation revealed – other than his having been killed in the first place – was that he had been drawing large amounts of money on both his personal and business accounts and nobody, not his wife, not the company's accountant nor anybody else had any idea where it had gone or what it had been for.

So, it could have been, as they say, a bastard of a case; no motive, no suspects, no nothing . . . except or one real stroke of luck, and that was the German ourist who had had wit enough to get busy with his amera. He was prevailed upon to allow the police to develop the film for him and what lovely photographs they turned out to be! Not much in the way of composition or framing, perhaps; not always quite in focus, sometimes even a bit blurred, owing to the haste and excitement of the moment; but what he had caught, in shot after shot, clear as day, was the registration number of that Volvo.

According to Swansea, it was registered in the name of one Norman James Price; and Norman James Price had form. In his thirty-seven years, Price had been done for a bit of just about everything, nicking cars, dishonestly handling, deception, living off immoral earnings, procuring, drug peddling, wounding, being in possession of an offensive weapon – namely a shotgun the barrels of which had been illegally shortened – resisting arrest, conspiracy to rob, conspiracy to defraud . . . He was, you could say, a good all-rounder; thoroughly and irretrievably bent. Rockliffe knew him, Flight knew him, half the CID officers in the Met knew him; about the only thing anyone could find to say in his favour was that whatever he turned his hand to, he never turned out to be spectacularly good at it – hence his record sheet, as long as anyone's arm.

Now it was murder, although according to Karen and Georgiou after they had seen the photographs of him, it was not Price but his overweight friend who had been carrying the gun and had pointed it at them. So presumably it had also been his overweight friend who actually shot Peter Thorne. That bothered Rockliffe; Price was nasty enough, but he had never been mad enough to go all the way before. But on the evidence they had, this unknown Mr Overweight seemed to have no compunction about it, which made him even nastier.

The first priority, however, was to find Price. Chances of his being at his home address were minimal.

or at the pub where he supposedly worked. They would be raided, of course, but no one had much hope of finding him or anything else of any real interest at either place. But then they had a second stroke of luck. Information was received – which meant that a grass had done some talking – that Price had a cousin who owned a car breakers and scrap yard in Dent Lane. And that, according to this grass, was where Price was lying low until the scream over Thorne's murder died down.

In the light of this information, Munro called a full operational briefing attended by the whole of the Crime Squad plus another dozen or so CID and uniformed officers. The Incident room was crowded, people having to sit on desks or lounge against the walls. At the front, behind Munro, there was a board on which a large-scale plan of the breakers yard and the streets around it had been pinned, along with several blow-ups of the German tourist's photographs featuring the Volvo. Rockliffe had also been caught on a couple of them, throwing his stick and charging after the car. There was something almost Chaplinesque about the way he looked: absurd and furious and impotent. There had been *sotto voce* comments and little ripples of unkind laughter which, stoically, he had borne and ignored.

'So much for the pub and Price's home,' Munro was saying. 'But the snout's told us our best chance is the car breakers, which is here,' he pointed with his stick, 'in the middle of Dent Lane just before the railway bridge. So I intend to lead the third group, concentrating on the yard. It's surrounded on two sides by a brick wall, and corrugated iron on the other two, topped with barbed wire. The main gate's here, in Dent Lane. There's also a small latchgate set into this wall here. So: here,' he pointed again, 'I would like

Sergeant Rockliffe and PCs Harrison and Wilson-Smith, covering the latchgate. And, er . . .' He proceeded with the disposition of his troops, managing to get the odd name wrong and to convey the impression of a general who has just slightly more regard for himself and his tactical ability than the men on the ground might consider altogether warranted.

'PCs Adams and . . . yes, O'Dowd, I want you up on the roof of the yard office to cover any possible escape through the skylight. Not likely but possible, if he's desperate enough.'

'Me, sir?' O'Dowd queried. 'On the roof?'

'Yes. Any objections?'

'No . . . well, yes, actually, like . . .'

'Don't argue, O'Dowd,' DI Flight interjected wearily.

'He suffers from vertigo, sir,' Adams informed them.

'First I've heard of it,' Munro said sharply and looked to Rockliffe. It was the first he had heard of it, too.

'Fell out of his pram at six months,' Georgiou enlightened them. 'Never got over the shock.'

'Hey, come on, it's not funny . . .' O'Dowd tried to plead in all seriousness, but he was drowned out by the cries of 'Aargh!' and laughter from the others.

'On the roof, O'Dowd,' Munro repeated.

O'Dowd caught Georgiou's eye and glared at him. Georgiou just winked.

'Now let's not forget – we've been very lucky so far,' Munro was concluding. 'First the tourist's photographs of Price's Volvo and now the snout. So let's keep it that way. Price may be in a corner, he's unpredictable and violent and he may, himself, be armed. So, no heroics. A neat, professional job and no casualties, that's what I'm after. Right. Let's do it.'

'Come on, Gerry,' Adams said, as they joined the

movement for the door. 'Just don't look down, that's the thing.'

'Great,' O'Dowd muttered dubiously. 'Hey, how do we get up there? . . .'

If he had known, he would have liked the idea even less . . .

They congregated in dribs and drabs at irregular intervals so that it took nearly twenty minutes before everyone was in position. Eventually, outside the yard and hidden from sight of the yard office windows, there were five cars, a dog van and a Transit. One of the police marksmen was on top of the Transit which gave him the height to fire comfortably over the yard wall. The second had slipped into the yard via the latchgate and was positioned near the top of a veritable mountain of tyres. Both were armed with Parker Hale rifles with telescopic sights through which they discreetly scanned the windows of the office, looking for tell-tale movement within.

Other officers besides the marksman had infiltrated the site, six or seven, slipping in through the gates and filing silently between the heaps of seemingly precariously balanced car shells which were dented and flattened and twisted and all the colours one could think of, but mostly just red with rust. Munro climbed out of his car and went to join Flight who was just outside the gates, watching the men's stealthy progress across the yard.

'So where is he, Charlie?' Munro asked.

Flight pointed to one of the first-floor windows in the building forty yards away. 'That one, we think. Under the window.' It was a brick building with half its windows broken and looked nearly as derelict as the cars.

'Shots?' Munro asked, meaning the marksmen.

Flight nodded to the man on top of the Transit, just

beyond the gates. 'Can't see the other from here,' he said. 'He's got himself behind a mound of tyres over there.'

Munro nodded. 'Everyone in position, then?'

''Part from the two on the roof,' Flight told him. 'No sign of them yet.'

Munro sighed. 'They've had long enough.'

Which, in O'Dowd's opinion, was neither true nor fair. Because the only way up on to the roof, from the rear, at least, had turned out to be up a drainpipe. And at just about the moment Munro was questioning their whereabouts, he was approximately two-thirds of the way up it. And he was sweating buckets.

'Nearly there, sir,' Adams told Munro over his PR, 'just another minute.' Then he lent over the parapet to see how O'Dowd was doing. 'Come on, Gerry,' he whispered hoarsely. 'They're waiting for us.'

'Okay,' O'Dowd muttered back through clenched teeth. 'Let 'em wait.' His eyes were tight shut. He was hugging that drainpipe like it was the dearest thing to him in all the world, which, at that moment, it very nearly was. His upward progress was so slow as to be virtually invisible to the naked eye. You would have needed time-lapse photography to convince yourself that he actually was moving at all.

'Come on,' Adams hissed. 'You don't want them starting without us in position .. .'

'I don't care,' O'Dowd said. 'Let 'em start.'

'You've nearly made it,' Adams encouraged him. 'Don't look down, look up at me . . .'

'I'm not looking anywhere,' O'Dowd told him. 'Just shut up an' tell me how I'm doing.'

'Great,' Adams said, 'I can nearly reach you.'

'Don't! . . .' O'Dowd exclaimed. 'Don't touch me . . .'

'Be easy going down,' Adams said, trying to give him heart.

'Shurrup about going down!' O'Dowd begged.

'No, I mean we'll be able to use the skylight,' Adams said.

'That a promise?' O'Dowd asked.

He had just about reached the parapet and Adams reached over to grab O'Dowd's arm. The shock of this contact gave O'Dowd such a start he gave a cry and almost lost his grip on the drainpipe. Adams grabbed hold of him and hauled, and in a terrified, scrambling rush O'Dowd came up, over the parapet and on to the roof to end up shaking with fright at Adams's feet.

'You shouldn't've done that,' he said.

'Oh come on,' Adams said impatiently, and started across the roof towards the skylight, while at the same time pulling out his PR to announce that they were now in position. Almost immediately, from the other side of the building, they heard Munro's voice coming at them through a loudhailer.

'Price? Norman Price? We know you're in there, Price. Take a look out of the window. You'll see me and my men all over the yard. There are also two marksmen who you can't see, and they have been given orders to fire if necessary. Okay? First open the window and throw down any firearm in your possession. Then leave the office, come down the stairs and out of the door. Walk across the yard with your hands up until you are standing where I am standing now. No tricks, Price. You are completely surrounded and any resistance would be futile. Do as I have said *now*, Price.'

Adams had gone to the parapet along the front of the building and was looking down.

'Gerry,' he called back. 'Come over here and look at Marylin.'

'I'm fine here, ta,' O'Dowd returned, still shaking slightly.

'Price! . . .' They heard Munro's voice again. 'Open the window, Price!'

'Dave,' O'Dowd said, 'suppose he comes up, like, through there,' he nodded to the skylight. 'What do we do?'

'Overpower him, of course.'

'Right,' said O'Dowd. 'Tell you what: you nick him an' I'll read him the caution.'

Adams gave him a jaundiced look, then returned his attention to what was happening down below. After a moment, he said, 'No need anyway. He's giving himself up. Crossing the yard now.'

'Oh is he?' said O'Dowd. 'Oh. Shame.'

But it was true. Price had appeared from the door of the building, arms held high and was crossing with an insolent kind of casualness towards Munro. The police marksmen were covering him through their telescopic sights every inch of the way.

'What's all the shenanigans, then?' he asked innocently.

'Where's your shooter, Price?' Munro demanded.

'I ain't got no shooter. Haven't had one in years.'

'Lie down with your arms out and your legs apart.'

Price did as he was ordered. Munro turned to Georgiou. 'Search him.' Georgiou did so. Price was definitely not carrying. 'Get up,' Munro ordered. Price clambered back to his feet and looked around at all the policemen surrounding him. He nodded to Rockliffe and then to Flight, acknowledging old acquaintance. He seemed infuriatingly, disgustingly nonchalant about the whole business.

'Norman Price,' Munro informed him, 'I am arresting you in connection with the murder of Peter Thorne at the Romney Hotel, yesterday morning. You do not have to say anything unless you wish to do so, but anything you do say may be given in evidence.' Price said nothing.

'Count up the number of times he's heard that caution,' Rockliffe thought, 'and one thing's for sure: you'd run out of fingers.'

'Who's your fat friend, Price?' Munro asked.

Price looked as though he hadn't the faintest idea what Munro was talking about.

'Take him away,' Munro said.

Up on the roof, O'Dowd had steeled himself to look down and saw Price being marched, handcuffed, out of the gates to one of the waiting cars. Some of the police officers were also departing while others began towards the offices to search them.

'Waste of time,' he said. 'Us coming up here.'

'Yeah,' Adams agreed, unhappily. O'Dowd looked round. Adams was squatting by the skylight, trying to raise it, with a conspicuous lack of success. He caught O'Dowd's look. 'Stuck,' he said regretfully, 'so we're going to have to go back down the drainpipe.'

O'Dowd looked sick. 'No,' he said. 'You go. I'll just wait here for the fire brigade.'

13

Events had somewhat overshadowed Eric Sinclair and the luggage thefts, but Rockliffe had not forgotten about him. Indeed, having so narrowly missed him on the morning of Thorne's murder he was all the more determined to have him, and all the rest of that clan of rogues; for brother Billy was the fence who punted Eric's gear and Tina, Billy's common-law wife . . . well, she was Tina, a very capable and loyal young lady who would do just about anything to help Billy, laying herself open to a rich variety of charges.

There was no knowing when Eric would next pull the luggage trick. After his narrow shave the other morning he might decide not to push his luck for a while; besides which, the tourist season was just about over for this year – till Christmas, anyway, and by then he'd be on a different scam entirely. So Rockliffe had decided not to wait for another tip-off but to take the fight to the enemy. They would raid the Sinclairs' house; in their own parlance, spin the Sinclairs' drum.

He hardly had enough bodies to bring it off. Chitty was on leave in Dorset while Karen and Georgiou, the only two to have had clear sight of the fat man with the gun, were seconded more or less permanently to the murder investigation. That left himself, Adams, O'Dowd, Hood and Janice. Hood was tied up waiting to give evidence in a case of attempted robbery, and Janice was supposed to be off sick after the shunt in the Astra. That cut on her hand had proved to be no mere graze. He needed her, though; because if they lifted Tina, there was the problem of what to do about her little daughter, Chantelle. Regulations and common sense required that a female officer should be present so, bandaged hand or no, she had to be hauled in, at least for the raid.

The Sinclairs lived in a street of crumbling Edwardian terraced houses which, over the last year or two, had grown discernibly shorter as one house after another became uninhabitable and the tenants moved out for the demolition men to move in. There were now only three or four families still living there. The rest of the houses still standing were boarded against squatters and vandalism – though not, as Rockliffe had discovered, all that effectively. To start with, he was inside one with Janice, and they clearly weren't the first. The walls were daubed with graffiti, mostly either political or obscene, and there was evidence on the floor of small camp fires having been lit. There was also a profusion of empty bottles suggesting that a colony of winos had, at some point, been in residence. The smell of the place, urine and decay and even the lingering tang of pot, was nauseous.

Across the street, almost directly opposite, was the Sinclairs' house with the Alpine parked at the kerb. The milkman had been; the paper boy had been; Tina had made one appearance on the step, still in her nightie, to bring in the milk bottles. Behind her they had heard Chantelle crying and the noise of Billy's rottweiler dog as it barked in response. Tina had shouted at it to shut up and the front door had closed again. Now Rockliffe waited for the Post Office van to appear.

It came slowly down the street, Adams at the wheel and O'Dowd beside him, both in Post Office uniforms. Outside the Sinclairs' house it double parked beside the Alpine and O'Dowd clambered out, carrying two bulky parcels. His uniform was a shade too large and he looked faintly comic as he flapped around the van towards the front door. Rockliffe sucked in his breath in a hiss of anxiety. He glanced back to Janice. 'Let's go,' he said.

Shielded from view of the house by the tall van, they squeezed out through a gap in the crudely boarded door and ran across to wait in the lee of the van's side. They could hear O'Dowd knocking on the door, and then the door being opened.

This time it was Billy, a big, friendly-looking West Indian in his middle thirties, who stood there. 'What's this?' he asked.

'Two registered parcels for Mr Sinclair,' O'Dowd told him. 'Are you Mr . . . Er, William Sinclair?'

Billy nodded. 'Early, ain't you?' he observed.

'We could call back later, if it's inconvenient . . .'

Billy eyed the parcels. 'No, it's okay. Where do I sign?'

'Just here, see?' O'Dowd was offering him the pad. 'Number Three and then again on Number Four.'

'Where they from, Billy?' Tina called from the hallway behind him.

O'Dowd juggled the parcels to look at the post marks. 'Tunbridge Wells and . . . Tunbridge Wells! You gotta fan club down there or something?'

Behind the van, Rockliffe grimaced with annoyance. O'Dowd was overdoing it.

Billy had taken the pad and pen and, leaning against the door jamb, he was signing where O'Dowd had indicated. He was off balance and off guard. Taking a deep breath, O'Dowd yelled, 'Right!! . . .' And dropping the parcels he pushed Billy backwards and tripped him.

On hearing the shout, Rockliffe and Janice erupted around from the side of the van and pelted for the doorway. Adams leapt from the driver's seat and followed. Down the hallway they vaguely heard Tina yelling, 'Billy?! . . .'

It was pandemonium. Billy was on the floor.

O'Dowd was charging for the kitchen. Tina was screaming and Billy was yelling, 'Clear off, Eric!! It's the pigs!!'

Rockliffe and Adams landed on Billy and started trying to cuff him. Janice kept on going, heading for the stairs. O'Dowd flung open the kitchen door and was in time to see Eric, wearing only his underpants and trainers, taking off through the back door and down the garden. Between O'Dowd and pursuit stood a huge, growling rottweiler who bared its teeth at O'Dowd and made a lunge towards him. O'Dowd backed out of the kitchen and slammed the door again a good deal faster than he had gone in.

Tina was still screaming, 'Bastards! Bastards!' while Rockliffe and Adams were still trying to subdue Billy who had managed to regain his feet, lifting them with him. Adams gave one of Billy's knees a sharp thwack with his stick and Billy collapsed again. O'Dowd headed up the stairs after Janice. In the kitchen, the rottweiler was barking and throwing itself against the door.

Upstairs, in the front bedroom, Janice had found Chantelle. She was standing in her cot, the bedlam downstairs clearly frightening and bewildering her, although she was not actually crying. She was a pretty little girl, hair in pigtails, with huge, serious eyes.

'Hello,' Janice said. 'I'm Janice. Are you Chantelle? You are, aren't you?' She picked up Chantelle's teddy from inside the cot. 'Is this your teddy? Shall we take Teddy with us? He's great, isn't he?' She persuaded the little girl to hold the teddy bear and then gently she lifted her out of the cot. 'Let's get your dressing gown, shall we?'

Out on the landing O'Dowd had tried the door of one of the other bedrooms. He was hardly prepared for what he saw: it was a veritable Aladdin's cave; videos, televisions, car radios, personal stereos, fur coats, leather jackets, a whole cardboard box full of quartz watches . . . O'Dowd slowly moved on into the room, giving a low whistle as he did so. What a haul! . . .

Something moved. Out of the corner of his eye he caught it, behind the bed, a rising motion . . . It was a second rottweiler, which sprang on to the bed and bared its teeth at him, a growl building in its throat. O'Dowd froze.

At about the same moment, Janice was reaching the bottom of the stairs and Tina saw what she was carrying: her little daughter.

'No!' she screamed. 'You're not taking my kid!!' and she launched herself towards Janice.

With Billy now cuffed, Rockliffe reckoned he could leave him to Adams and he threw himself after Tina, dragging her away from Janice and the child who mutely watched these proceedings through wide, startled eyes. Janice quickly headed for the front door leaving Rockliffe struggling with Tina. It was like fighting a wild animal. She twisted, kicked, spat, scratched, writhed and bucked while all the time shrieking, 'No! No! No! Bastards! Bastards!! You're not taking my kid!!'

Rockliffe wasn't sure he could hold her. 'O'Dowd!' he yelled. 'O'Dowd!!'

O'Dowd could hear his name being shouted and he recognized the urgency, but right now was not the best moment for him to respond because any sudden move, he reckoned, and that dog's teeth would be ripping out his laughing tackle – or worse. Very, very gently he was sliding out his stick, while the dog continued to growl and to set him.

'Good dog,' O'Dowd ventured. 'Good dog . . .'

'O'Dowd!!!' he heard Rockliffe yelling.

O'Dowd slowly extended the stick towards the dog. Its growl was building, the spring in its body growing more taut. Suddenly it barked, lunged and seized the stick, which is what O'Dowd had been banking on. With its mouth thus occupied, even if only for a moment, it gave him time to rush out of the room and slam the door.

He came down the stairs two at a time, to find Rockliffe and Tina engaged in something that looked the next best thing to all-in wrestling. 'Grab hold!' Rockliffe yelled. O'Dowd entered the fray and between them, gradually, they subdued her. 'She'll be alright, Tina,' Rockliffe tried to reassure her.

'Bastards!' she said. 'Bastards.' And she began to cry.

By the time they reached the station everyone was a little bit calmer and Billy, in particular, didn't seem to be holding any ill feelings against them. Indeed, as Adams searched for the letters to put on the slat which would identify Billy on their photo of him, he couldn't have been more helpful. It seemed as though he knew the Fingerprint room better than Adams did himself.

'Over there,' he advised. 'More letters an' that. In that top drawer, over there. Used to be.'

And, indeed, they still were. Adams got the slat set up while Billy sat impassively on the stool in front of the camera.

'Sorry about the knee,' Adams apologized.

''S alright,' Billy forgave him. 'All's fair in love an' war.' He laughed.

'And which is ours, I wonder?' Adams mused.

'War, baby,' Billy told him emphatically. 'I'm a prisoner of war.'

'Yes, I'm rather coming to the same conclusion,' Adams admitted. He peered through the viewfinder and adjusted the focus.

'What you study then, at university?' Billy asked.

'Anthropology. Totem poles and things.'

'Yeah,' Billy said. 'I do know long words.' He regarded Adams for a moment in an amused, quizzical sort of way. 'Only now, you're a pig. Why?! They're all thick, man. No one with brains should be a pig!'

Which quite stumped Adams. He had to think for several moments. 'Well, er . . . I suppose I prefer working outdoors. And er . . . I wanted to meet ordinary people. And help them if possible.' He was uncomfortably aware that in the present context that sounded feeble and even risible.

Billy just said, 'Jee-suss!' And roared his head off.

In the interview room, however, confronting Rockliffe and Janice, Tina was in no such laughing mood. 'What've you done with her?' she demanded.

'She's fine, Tina,' Janice assured her. 'I told you. They're keeping her at Lockerby Terrace till you're released.'

'That the home?'

'Yeah. She's got a cot, and more toys than she can play with.'

Tina lit herself a cigarette with trembling fingers. ''S not right, you know. Stop at nothing, you Crime Squad lot. Every dirty trick in the book. She could've gone to Billy's Mum, if you'd asked.'

'There wasn't time to ask, Tina,' Janice said gently.

'Don't you "Tina" me, you little cow!' Tina flared.

'Hey-up! . . .' Rockliffe intervened, thinking that was a little uncalled for.

'My name's Mrs Sinclair,' Tina persisted, regardless. 'What're you doing with this crowd, anyway?'

'How d'you mean?' Janice asked.

'You know what I mean,' she was told. 'Traitor, you are!'

'Now that's enough, Tina!' Rockliffe intervened once more. 'Just settle down, have your fag and get a grip on yourself, okay?' Tina puffed in angry silence for a moment. Janice rose and, catching Rockliffe's eye,

112

pointed to the ceiling. 'Aye,' he said, 'yes, I will.' He looked to Tina. 'How about you? Tea, coffee, what?'

'Coffee,' she said. 'Milk and no sugar.'

'Right.' Janice moved towards the door.

'Oh, and one of them Eccles cakes, if they still do them, love.' It seemed she had decided to call off the war. Janice nodded and went.

Between Rockliffe and Tina there was a pause, not awkward, almost companionable, in fact. She was a pretty girl, Rockliffe had always thought, when she wasn't trying to tough it out; given a different start, a few less bad breaks, who was to know how different her life might have been? But even as he thought it he also knew that given a choice, she wouldn't have things any other way. Except maybe right now.

'You got back with your wife?' Tina asked. Rockliffe shook his head with a tiny, rueful smile. 'Thought not. Your collar's filthy.'

'Ah.' Rockliffe nodded. 'No, still up in Leicester. Never come back now. It's the kid I miss. She's down tomorrow, for the weekend . . . That's what I get. One weekend in twenty and be thankful. And I am thankful, aye.' And this weekend was special: he thought of the bracelet, now wrapped; he'd even managed to fancy up the ribbon a bit for her. The tickets for the theatre; a meal afterwards. Eighteen years old; she was a big girl now, grown up – all of a sudden, somehow, without him really noticing. And she was pretty, too; like her mother had been, before she'd married him. He found himself wondering whether that was what had done it, whether it was being married to him, particularly to him, that had lost Kate's mother her looks. Then he found himself imagining the glances they'd get, him and Kate together, at the theatre and in the restaurant, from other blokes and from couples who wouldn't know that she was his daughter; some of them would take

113

her for his fancy bit; and that made him feel angry and confused. His daughter, some bloke's fancy woman. Christ, it could happen . . .

He looked back to Tina. 'You still tomming?'

'When the mood takes me. And the law lets me.'

'Where?'

'Up and down and round about. Paddington mostly. Street hustling – the usual. Some things never change.'

'And Billy's your ponce?'

Tina laughed scornfully. 'Come off it, Rockliffe. Don't try that one. I ain't got no ponce, them days are long gone.'

'If he eats a crumb off the end of your loaf,' Rockliffe told her, 'he's your ponce.'

'Oh really? That I never knew,' she said contemptuously. 'Never had class, did you? No wonder you got nowhere.'

Rockliffe didn't respond. He thoughtfully stoked his pipe, then rose to stretch his legs.

'What can I do with you, eh, Tina?' he asked reasonably. 'On a suspended for kiting, turning tricks in Paddington, houseful of bent gear, refuses to answer questions. What can I tell the judge? Your tax is up good and proper, Tina.'

'I know nothing,' she threw back at him. 'I done nothing. What Billy gets up to is his own business. It's his house, not mine. I never fenced nothing. So just let me go and get my kid.' Rockliffe slowly shook his head. 'What d'you *want*, Rockliffe?' she demanded.

'Eric,' he said simply.

'Oh no! Oh no!' She was shaking her head. 'What d'you think I am?' She laughed at the absurdity of what he was asking.

'Suppose Billy goes down for a stretch this time,' he said. 'Suppose you do. You think they're going to let you have the kid back when you get out? You think they're going to consider you a fit parent?'

She hated him! She *hated* him! But what could she do? He had the system and pure, good, upright, righteous society all on his side. And everything he had said would come to pass without him even needing to lift a finger. It galled her beyond words. Whereas, to stop it happening, she had to make it worth him lifting his finger. Officially, it was forbidden, it was denied, it didn't happen. Only in rooms like this, between people like them, when the tape recorder was switched off and there weren't any witnesses, then blackmail was alive and well in this land! . . . Blackmail!! . . .

'I've got a name,' she said. Rockliffe nodded approvingly. 'Only it's not to do with Billy. Or Eric. I'd never grass on them, never. Even if I knew and I tell you I don't know. Not even for the kid, and she's my life, Rockliffe.'

'So who is it to do with?' Rockliffe asked quietly.

'Peter Thorne. The guy who got shot.'

The surprise stopped Rockliffe short in his tracks. 'You knew him?!'

'We all did. The girls, I mean.'

'He was a punter? . . .'

'Kind of, yeah. Only I couldn't do nothing for him. He had this kink, see, and I couldn't help him. Only this other feller could. But then he took some photographs and started blackmailing him – well, hardly the word for it. Stripping him clean more like.'

'Thorne told you this?'

She nodded. 'When he was found, did he have a gun or a knife or anything?' Rockliffe shook his head. 'Oh.' She seemed almost disappointed. 'Only that's what *I'd* reckoned: that he'd decided to wipe 'em up 'stead of going on paying. Only they'd done him instead.'

'Maybe he'd threatened to come to us,' Rockliffe said.

She nodded with a small shrug. 'Maybe.'

'You said "them", "paying them". We've got Norman Price; so who's the other one?'

'Norman not singing?' Rockliffe shook his head. 'Can't say as I'm surprised. See, the other one, he's mental, right? Real nasty piece of work. Keeps a gun in his back pocket – says it was a present from a copper, someone in CID, years back. That's him, always boasting.'

'Called?' Rockliffe was almost holding his breath.

'McAteer.'

'Danny McAteer?'

She nodded. 'Friend of yours?'

Rockliffe didn't answer. He was too busy dealing with all the memories that name evoked. Danny McAteer! One-time Porn-King of Soho, with half the Dirty Books Squad on his payroll. And Rockliffe, poor, green, rookie Rockliffe, had one day actually nicked him. And had been practically cut off at the knees by his superiors for his trouble! Danny McAteer! And to think he had been that close, and he'd not recognized either of them – Price or McAteer. He shook his head to himself; he must be getting past it!

'Where can I find him?' he asked. She shrugged; she didn't know. 'So what was this kink that Thorne had that made him easy pickings to McAteer? Rent boys or summat?'

She shook her head. 'Short socks.'

Rockliffe nodded slowly. Yes; that was McAteer.

14

Price was having his evening meal when Rockliffe was admitted to the cell. He looked up and showed surprise.

'Hello, Rockliffe. Hey, you're not my brief. I was told my brief was coming.'

'Just called in to see how you are, Norman,' Rockliffe said pleasantly.

'That'll be the day,' Price replied. 'Too much salt.' He jabbed his spoon at the Irish Stew. 'In the stew. Too salty. And that's all I'm saying.'

Rockliffe watched him for a moment as he ate. The salt didn't seem to be spoiling his appetite. Price looked back at him, self-conscious all of a sudden. 'Here, what you staring at?' he demanded. 'Have I got two heads or something?'

'Where is he, Price?' Rockliffe asked quietly. 'Where can I find him?'

'Look, what's this all about?!' Price complained. 'I dunno what you're on about. I dunno what you're doing here, Rockliffe. I've been questioned for nine hours since yesterday. And now I'm sitting here having me nosh. Alright?'

He went to take another spoonful but suddenly the plate moved, as Rockliffe calmly lifted it from his knee and set it on the floor.

'Here! . . .' Price started to object, but didn't get any further because Rockliffe bodily lifted him from his seat and pinned him to the wall.

'Get this straight, Price,' Rockliffe said softly but clearly. 'I've only got one question for you, lad; and if you don't tell me the answer I'll paint you all over the walls of the bin – clear?' He shook Price hard. 'Clear?!'

'Let go!' Price said.

'Where is he?'

'Who?! . . .'

Rockliffe swung Price around, off his feet and on to the mattress, face down; then twisted his arm behind his back.

'You're busting my arm, you bloody animal! . . .' Price squealed.

'Not got it yet, have you, Price?' Rockliffe twisted some more. 'Now, where is he?'

'Who?!!'

'Danny!!' Rockliffe leant on him, increasing the pressure. 'I want an address, Price. Come on, come on, you're being slow, lad . . .' Price was crying with the pain. 'Sorry, sorry? Didn't catch that, didn't quite catch it.'

'Cinema club! . . .' Price yelled.

'Yes, good, go on. Cinema club, go on!'

'End of Lovell Parade. The Triple X, it's called. White an' red front! . . .'

Rockliffe abruptly let go of his arm and stepped back. Slowly Price squirmed over from his stomach and began to massage the arm where it hurt. Rockliffe rang the bell then waited, contemptuously regarding the prisoner. Price managed not to look back at him. The cell door swung open and the Custody Sergeant was there, looking very balefully at Rockliffe.

'Enjoy your dinner, Norman,' Rockliffe said, and went out.

He found Adams and O'Dowd as they were about to leave the squad office to go for a pint. He was thankful that he'd caught them. 'Oh good,' he said. 'You're both ready.'

'Ready?' Adams queried.

'I need you both for a job.'

It was the first they had heard of it, and they looked at each other, a bit taken aback and not exactly leaping with enthusiasm.

'Er, 'ey, Skip,' O'Dowd said, 'We've bin on the go since sparrow fart. What is this job?'

'To lift Thorne's killer.'

That really threw them. They looked at each other again, wondering what had happened, what he was rabbiting on about.

'I can't make you come,' Rockliffe admitted. 'And it'll be dangerous, because he's armed and we won't be. But I want him badly. Very badly. He's an old acquaintance, see?'

'How do you know who it is?' Adams asked, stunned.

'My business,' Rockliffe answered brusquely. 'Well? Yes or no?'

Neither of them responded for a moment, though Rockliffe was willing them to agree with all the power he had. He *wanted* their support; not just because McAteer was a mad bugger who had already killed one man and probably wouldn't hesitate to do so again. He just wanted their support, *their support*, on this; human being to human being, teacher to pupil and pupil to teacher, he wanted them to back him, freely and of their own volition, as badly as he wanted McAteer's collar. Still neither of them responded.

'Okay,' he said. 'Go on my own, then. Goodnight.'

But he hadn't even got as far as the door before he heard them hurrying after him. He grinned to himself, with triumph and relief and gratitude. But he made damn bloody sure neither of them saw it.

The cinema club was exactly where Price had said it was, neon lights rippling and flashing across its red and white façade. The bloke on the door was very accommodating; at the first sight of their warrant cards he simply thrust violently past them and took off into the Soho night showing the cleanest pair of heels since Steve Cram had run at Crystal Palace. They glanced at each other in wry, grim amusement, then pushed on down the dim, musty corridor.

They passed a pair of double doors from behind which they could hear repetitive, throbbing, grinding rock music which was presumably the sound-track accompaniment of the film that was running. Buried within it they could hear a woman's gasps and moans, grossly overdone.

'Knew a bird who used to do that,' O'Dowd informed them in a whisper.

'What? . . .' said Adams, shocked.

'Sound effects. Actress, she was at the Liverpool Playhouse. Told me they dub all the sound effects on after. Hysterical, her an' a feller standing fully clothed either side of a mike, watchin' the movie an' making them noises at each other. Can you imagine it?'

'No,' Adams said.

'Shut up,' Rockliffe warned them. They had come to the end of the passage where there was a door marked 'Private'. He paused. 'Know what to do? We're all clear?' O'Dowd and Adams both nodded. Rockliffe gently grasped the handle of the door, turned it and pushed the door open.

The room in which he and Adams found themselves was a small office, crudely converted to double as the projection room. The projector, flickering through a hole cut in the wall, afforded the only light, by which they could just make out the bulky figure of a man standing at the desk, piling money and papers into a suitcase. He looked up as they entered.

'Hello, Danny,' Rockliffe said.

'Who's that? . . .'

'Alan Rockliffe. Remember me?'

Rockliffe moved close to the projector so that some of the overspill light illuminated his face.

'Yeah,' McAteer said after a moment. 'I remember you.'

'This your business?' Rockliffe asked.

'Nah,' McAteer said. 'Run it for the Maltese geezer who's never here. You still Old Bill?'

'That's right. Nothing much changes, does it? This is one of my men.'

'Oh yeah?' There was a pause. 'You look old, Rockliffe.'

'Going somewhere?' Rockliffe asked. He nodded to the suitcase.

'Austria.'

'Bit early for skiing, isn't it?'

'Is it? Ta for the tip.' McAteer closed the case, snapped the locks and, lifting it from the desk, started to make a move towards the door.

'No, Danny,' Rockliffe said. ''Cos you're nicked.'

'What?! For showing blue rollers?!' McAteer gave an unpleasant laugh. 'This place is licensed, didn't you check? It's all legal an' above board . . .'

'For resisting arrest, Danny,' Rockliffe said, interrupting him. 'See, when you shot Thorne two days ago, I was the one who threw the truncheon at the back window of Price's car. Only you didn't stop. Which is an arrestable offence, I'll have you know. Let's have some light, Adams.'

Adams' hand groped for the light switch by the door. When the light came on they were all momentarily blinded. By the time Rockliffe and Adams were able to see again McAteer had his gun in his hand and was covering them.

'Never got it right, did you, Rockliffe?' he sneered. He used the gun to motion Adams away from the door. Adams carefully obliged. McAteer moved over to the door and, keeping his gun on the two policemen, inched the door open to look down the passage. It was clear. 'You come after me, you both get one,' he said. 'Understood?' Neither of them said anything, but neither did they move. McAteer opened the door wide and stepped out into the passage, whereupon Rockliffe and Adams, noisily, lunged after him. McAteer heard them and swung back. Adams was to the fore and the gun was starting to lift towards him as O'Dowd, as though from nowhere, suddenly erupted from the doorway of the stinking gents loo just behind McAteer and threw himself upon him. McAteer, taken by surprise and already off balance, buckled. In the next instant Adams was also upon him, wresting the gun from his hand and twisting back his arm for O'Dowd to snap on the handcuffs.

Rockliffe stood regarding him as they allowed him to stumble back to his feet. With satisfaction he saw that the fat man was now suddenly sweating. 'Now you're going to take us, Danny,' he said evenly, 'to your little nest. Where've you got 'em, Danny?'

For a moment it looked as though McAteer might even defy him yet. But then the last shreds of resistance seeped out of him. 'The Dragon,' he said thickly.

So it was back to The Dragon. Amazing how many investigations started or ended here; how many roads led in this one direction. In Victorian times there had been the rookeries, honeycombed mazes of tenements and stinking hovels into which the then custodians of the law did not and dared not penetrate. In Rockliffe's time there was the Dragon; and he did.

The flat was on the third floor of one of the tower blocks. The door had a peep-hole and a sliding hatch. The woman who admitted them, sour and frightened, was in her forties, answered to the name of Iris but was no flower and probably never had been. The room they were looking for – the nest – was at the end of the bare, scruffy passage. Rockliffe sent Adams and

O'Dowd to suss it out. He didn't want to; he had seen it all before and it turned his stomach over. But they hadn't; and it was time they did.

Inside the room there was a bed, a dressing table, a wardrobe and two chairs, none of them matching. The window was boarded up. On the bed sat a man in his shirt and trousers, in his fifties, overweight, balding. With him were two girls. The elder, naked, was lying on the bed. The younger, wearing just a man's shirt and short white socks was sitting beside him. Her mouth was grotesquely emphasized with loud lipstick. Both of the girls giggled at Adams and O'Dowd because both of them were stoned to high heaven. The elder would be about fourteen, Adams reckoned; the younger no more than eleven. The man on the bed took in the two young coppers, then slowly buried his face in his hands.

'This time you go down and you stay down,' Rockliffe told McAteer. 'And if I didn't know that, I think I'd do for you now.'

15

'What's his name again?' asked Detective Chief Inspector Munro.

'McAteer, sir,' Rockliffe told him. 'Danny McAteer.'

Munro nodded slowly. He was getting the measure of Rockliffe, and it was a measure he didn't like. He didn't like glory hunters, he didn't like cowboys, and he didn't like individualists running private initiatives with their own private army, particularly not when it was his case. Standing in front of him, Rockliffe could sense the displeasure, the censure and the cold hostility in the other man.

'When did you come by this information?'

'Earlier today. From a snout.'

'Is that why you went to see Price in his cell?'

'Yes. I had a name, but not where he hung out. I knew Price could tell us.'

'Us? You, you mean!'

'I did obtain Sergeant Oates's permission to visit Price, and he did ring you first. But you weren't in your office and it seemed necessary to act quickly.'

Munro gave off one of those – by now – famous laughs of his, a single, humourless bark.

'Did you arrest him on your own?'

'No. I asked two of my best men if they'd volunteer to come with me. Which they duly did.'

'Did you warn them McAteer would be armed?'

'Of course. And they acted with great courage in the course of the arrest.'

'Two unarmed, rookie constables, to collar a known villain who'd shot an innocent man two days ago? . . .'

'Innocent?' Rockliffe lightly queried. 'We've got the shooter, by the way. It's a police special.'

'You what? . . .' Munro said.

'It was a present to him, from an Inspector in the Department many years ago. A Christmas present.'

'God damn you, Rockliffe,' Munro thought, 'you enjoyed telling me that; you're subversive, you're undisciplined, and you're a bloody bad influence on those rookies.' 'That was in the bad old days, Rockliffe,' he said, managing not to betray his thoughts. 'They're over now.'

'Yeah,' Rockliffe said. 'Except . . .'

'Except what?'

'Except that Inspector's now a Commander.'

It was almost deliberate, Munro thought, almost rehearsed; a deliberate slap in the face, deliberately provoking, deliberately disrespectful. 'You hate us, don't you?' he said quietly. 'You really hate us. Except you're one of us. So I take it, Sergeant, you also hate yourself?'

'I've got my body,' was all Rockliffe replied.

Munro rose slowly and went over to the window, staring balefully out at the car lights and the shop lights and the glow in the sky that betokened a great city. His reflection in the glass was insubstantial, shadowy and spectral. 'We've almost lost the war,' he said flatly, 'down there. You know that, don't you?'

'Aye,' Rockliffe agreed.

'Every night, the termites come out. Boring deeper into the wood. The house won't stand much longer, that's my honest opinion. Some time in the next five years, ten if we're lucky, it'll suddenly fall down. And they'll all blame us: the politicians, the blessed British public. We've got no one on our side, sergeant, nothing going for us. Nothing.' He turned abruptly. 'Except – discipline. Discipline! If you were younger and had a future I'd roast you over hot coals for this. But you don't care, do you? Not any more. Water off a duck's back, far as you're concerned. The Crime Squad is not your private army! And you do not use it, *ever*, to settle old scores! Understood? And, by Christ, Rockliffe, if ever we talk again, in here, alone, or out there, you'll damn well call me Sir!!'

Rockliffe regarded him without expression. And said nothing.

It was yet later. But a light still shone in the Crime Squad office and Rockliffe still sat at his desk. He knew that the others were all over at the boozer, waiting for him to come and join them for a pint. It touched him, that; the way they had asked him – for his sake, not theirs. But he wouldn't go. Not now. Not after his phone call.

So she wasn't coming. She'd been invited to a party, close friend and all that, someone he actually remembered from days so long ago it was like remembering an earlier incarnation. Felt she couldn't miss it; sorry and all that, hoped he hadn't gone to too much trouble. The theatre tickets, still in the agency envelope, now lay on top of the day's trash in his bin.

Some other weekend, she had said; as though one weekend was as good as any other. It was only a duty visit, after all . . .

'I'll keep your present till you come, then,' Rockliffe had said pointedly.

'Oh – what is it?' she'd asked. 'Go on, Dad, tell me.'

'No chance,' he'd said. 'You want to find out, you turn up here.'

He rose from his desk, took down his mac and ambled slowly, heavily towards the door. He paused at an old 'wanted' poster for a moment, regarding the photofit features of some robber-*cum*-rapist, still at large, still somewhere out there.

'Sod the lot of you,' Rockliffe said, to Munro, to the Force, to every villain there ever was and to the world in general. But not to his Team; them he cared for.

He switched off the light and went out, slamming the door.